"Do you always giggle this much or only when you drink champagne?"

"Only when I drink champagne with handsome strangers," Drew said.

"Well played." His voice was a low murmur as he leaned in, his eyes touching her lips. He then sat back, taking her breath with him, and sipped his scotch while she drained half her champagne.

She suddenly didn't want this to be over. She didn't want the veil to fall away—for Reid to see her as Drew Fleming. She wanted to continue being charming and flirty and beautiful. She wanted to relax and have fun and flirt. Her gaze locked on that full lower lip and that contoured top lip and she couldn't get the idea out of her head that she should kiss him. Before it was too late. Before she lost her chance forever. Because as soon as he figured out that she was Drew, it would all be over.

A wave of panic sailed through her chest. She set aside her champagne and turned toward him.

"Tell me more about—" he started.

But she cut him off in the most delicious way imaginable. Her hands on either side of his disturbingly dashing face, she tugged his mouth to hers and kissed him long and hard.

* * *

One Night, White Lies is the third book of the Bachelor Pact series.

Dear Reader,

Reid Singleton is in for the shock of his life after he woos the sexy woman he flirted with at a work conference back to his hotel suite. You see, the "stranger" who allowed him to seduce her is none other than—insert dramatic music here—his best friend's little sister, Drew!

I had so, so, *so* much fun playing with the mistaken identity in this book. Drew had a huge crush on her older brother's best friend, but didn't have a prayer of snagging Reid's attention when she was younger. Now, with her new body and her newfound confidence, she lures Reid into her web...and she's not ready to let him go!

When these two start exploring their attraction, they find a mountain of compatibility underneath. But right when everything seems to be going perfectly, a shadow from Reid's past returns and throws everyone involved a curveball. Now he's faced with balancing the ghost from his past with the woman who could be his future... Can he handle them both?

Keep reading to find out...

xo,

Jessica Lemmon

Come see me at www.jessicalemmon.com.

Instagram: @jlemmony

Lemmondrops Superfans: Facebook.com/groups/lemmondrops

JESSICA LEMMON

ONE NIGHT, WHITE LIES

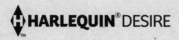

HARLEQUIN®DESIRE

Recycling programs
for this product may
not exist in your area.

ISBN-13: 978-1-335-60376-0

One Night, White Lies

Copyright © 2019 by Jessica Lemmon

Printed in U.S.A.

A former job-hopper, **Jessica Lemmon** resides in Ohio with her husband and rescue dog. She holds a degree in graphic design currently gathering dust in an impressive frame. When she's not writing supersexy heroes, she can be found cooking, drawing, drinking coffee (okay, wine) and eating potato chips. She firmly believes God gifts us with talents for a purpose, and with His help, you can create the life you want.

Jessica is a social media junkie who loves to hear from readers. You can learn more at jessicalemmon.com.

Books by Jessica Lemmon

Harlequin Desire

Dallas Billionaires Club

Lone Star Lovers
A Snowbound Scandal
A Christmas Proposition

The Bachelor Pact

Best Friends, Secret Lovers
Temporary to Tempted
One Night, White Lies

Visit her Author Profile page at Harlequin.com, or jessicalemmon.com, for more titles.

You can find Jessica Lemmon on Facebook, along with other Harlequin Desire authors, at Facebook.com/harlequindesireauthors!

For Aunt Beth.

Your passion for creating a life you love continues to inspire me to do the same.

One

$\underline{\qquad}$

London-born Reid Singleton didn't know a damn thing about women's shoes. So when he became transfixed by a pair on the dance floor, fashion wasn't his dominating thought.

They were pink, but somehow also metallic, with long Grecian-style straps crisscrossing delicate, gorgeous ankles. He curled his scotch to his chest and backed into the shadows, content to watch the woman who owned those ankles for a bit.

Reid might not know women's brands or styles, but he knew women. He'd seen quite a lot of women in high heels and short skirts, but he couldn't recall one who'd snagged his attention this thoroughly.

From those pinkish metallic spikes, the picture only improved. He followed the straps to perfectly rounded calves and the outline of tantalizing thighs lost in a skirt that moved when she did. The cream-colored skirt led to a sparkling gold top. Her shoulders were slight, the swells of her breasts snagging his attention for a beat, and her hair fell in curls over those small shoulders. Dark hair with a touch of mahogany, or maybe rich cherry. Not quite red, but with a notable amount of warmth, the way a tree ended its journey from burnished gold to deep russet in the fall.

He sipped from his glass, again taking in the skirt, both flirty and fun in equal measures. A guy could get lost in there. Get lost in *her*.

An inviting thought, indeed.

When the opportunity to attend a technology trade show in San Diego, California, arose, Reid leaped at the chance. He'd been on high alert for the past two years, ever since his best friend, Flynn, survived a divorce, his dad's death and elevation to president of his company all within a relatively short period of time. Reid worked at said company, liked his job, respected the hell out of Flynn and wasn't willing to step away until the situation was sorted.

This trip to California was looked upon as a break by Reid and a necessity by Flynn. They'd implemented a lot of changes in the past twelve months, and Reid was intent on making the tech side of the company shine. He was the self-appointed King of Information. Data made sense to him.

So did women.

The brunette spun around, her skirt swirling, her smile a seemingly permanent feature. She was lively and vivid, and even in her muted gold-and-cream ensemble, somehow the brightest color in the room. A man approached her, and Reid promptly lost his smile, a strange feeling of propriety rolling over him and causing him to bristle.

The suited man was average height with a receding hairline. He was on the skinny side, but the vision in gold simply smiled up at him, dazzling the man like he'd cast a spell. When she shook her head in dismissal and the man ducked his head and moved on, relief swamped Reid, but he still didn't approach her.

Careful was the only way to proceed, or so instinct told him. She was open but somehow skittish, in an outfit he couldn't take his eyes from. And he wasn't the only one looking. Upon a second glance around, he saw that there were, in fact, many men looking at her.

Most were in clusters with one another, clinging to their own. The company Reid worked for had sent him alone, atypical since he worked closely with his best friends from college, but he didn't mind flying solo. He was a *Single*ton, after all.

At Monarch Consulting, they shared the goal of helping other businesses grow and perform better. Flynn Parker—the aforementioned inheritor of the firm—was in charge and, while a bit straight-edged, definitely the best man for the job. Gage Fleming was in charge of sales, a good fit since he leaked charm like a noxious gas. Reid fancied himself a blend of both men, which was why they got on so well. The fourth musketeer, Sabrina Douglas, had been the bestie and plucky sidekick for years but recently became Flynn's wife-to-be. A kick in the nuts since Flynn was the one who initiated a pact with Gage and Reid never to wed in the first place.

But Reid couldn't deny that Sabrina and Flynn were meant to be together. It was obvious that they were in love, even to a cynic like Reid. Gage had agreed and they'd released Flynn from the pact, leaving Reid and Gage to hold strong.

Until Gage met Andrea Payne, a consultant superhero with strawberry-blond locks and a cunning smile. They were quite the dynamo couple, Andy and Gage. Their wedding was scheduled for next June. Flynn and Sabrina hadn't set an official date, but Reid guessed that announcement was forthcoming.

Weddings, weddings everywhere.

No matter. The breaking of the pact by both Flynn and Gage wasn't something Reid took personally. He'd decided a long time ago never to be married for a mountain of reasons he wasn't going to turn over in his head now. Gage's and Flynn's saying "I do" weren't going to change his mind.

Another swish of the brunette's skirt paired with her stepping from the dance floor. She aimed those tall shoes right for him. Reid reached up to straighten his tie, forgetting he'd tossed it on the bed in his hotel room along with his jacket. He settled for tugging his collar instead.

In his beige slacks, pale blue shirt, brown belt and brown leather shoes, he resembled every other man in the room save for a few slight differences.

Reid was thirty-one, not in his forties or fifties. He had a head full of wavy dark hair, no signs of male pattern baldness whatsoever. He also had a face that was perplexingly handsome, or so he'd been told. It was a face that aided him in bedding the many women who'd graced his sheets over the years, and he'd made it his mission to show them not just a good time but the *best* time while they were there.

Sabrina had once joked about Reid sleeping his way through their college campus. He'd responded that he'd been performing a service for women who otherwise wouldn't have known good sex if it showed up at their dorm room door wearing pasties on its nipples.

A joke, sure, but he hadn't been *completely* joking. He prided himself on his prowess as much as his service. He might be Clark Kent by day, glasses on when screen fatigue became too much, but at night he morphed into Superman in the bedroom.

Man of Steel, he thought with a smirk.

For those reasons he hadn't been in a rush to approach the goddess in the Grecian-style high heels like some of the other men in the room. Reid had already decided to carefully choose his moment, but as she made eye contact, he realized he wasn't going to have to approach her.

She was coming to him.

Two

Until this exact moment in time, Drew Fleming had never successfully captured Reid Singleton's undivided attention. She'd recognized him the instant their eyes locked across the room. He looked the same as when her brother, Gage, had introduced him years ago. To summarize: disgustingly, distractingly *hot*.

Reid, while *still* disgustingly, distractingly hot, was also somehow *more*. More mature. Slightly weathered. Handsome. Stately. Broader, too, his shoulders taking up more space in that button-up shirt than they had a right to.

Her heart pattered insistently against her rib cage as she walked toward him, and she forced herself to take deep breaths. She wasn't going to dissolve into Reid's biggest fan at a conference mixer, nor was she going to have a panic attack and run off in another direction. Drew was proud of who she was, of how far she'd come. She was no longer Gage's backward, chubby younger sister. She couldn't remember the last time she'd smiled shyly as she hid behind her hair.

She put a hop in her next step as she drew her chin up and shook her hair. Reid's tempting mouth slid into an expression that screamed *interested*. And who could blame him? She was *rocking* this skirt.

Reid and Drew didn't have much of a past to speak of, considering he'd only known her when she was fifty pounds heavier. She'd been the quiet girl sneaking frosting off the edge of her birthday cake because she couldn't wait for everyone to sing "Happy Birthday" before she tasted it.

Back then she'd had either white-blond hair with pink streaks, or jet black—that phase had lasted what felt like forever—before accepting her weight and her mouse-brown natural hair color as an adult. But today Reid was seeing her as her best self. Her rich, dark hair long and flowing over her shoulders. Her smile bright, her lipstick fresh, her new killer heels sexily laced up her ankles. If there was ever a perfect time to run into Reid Singleton, it was right now.

She'd have to call her roommate, Christina, the moment this mixer was over and thank her for coming down with the plague.

See, Drew might be herself, but she also *wasn't* herself. She was playing the role of her roommate, who'd had the unfortunate luck to contract the flu before the tech event for her company. Christina had been working at the Brentwood Corporation for just under a year and was worried if she missed the first conference they'd assigned her to, they'd never ask her to do another.

Drew was desperately in need of a break after a messy split with her ex a year ago. She felt was like she was emerging from the shadows after a long, deep slumber, so she volunteered to come here in Christina's stead.

Admittedly, manning—or *womanning*—the booth at the conference wasn't as fun as an *actual* vacation, but Drew made the best of it. She'd had a lot of visitors today and smiled and welcomed them even if she didn't understand what the heck the video she played on repeat was trying to convey. But what she was skilled at was small talk, and so whenever someone popped in, she'd winged it.

Tonight's mixer was a great excuse to wear the new shoes, admittedly a splurge, but she'd learned to spoil herself—to splurge on things *other* than food. Drew *splurged* on joy. *Splurged* on clothes. And tonight she might *splurge* on flirting with Reid Singleton. The way he was watching her hinted that he would enjoy that.

She ventured over to the quiet, darker part of the room only he was occupying. Reid set aside his glass, an inch of brown liquid in the bottom, and tilted his head as she approached.

She was tempted to duck her head to hide from the intense eye contact, but she forced herself to hold his cerulean gaze. "Hi."

"Hello." His voice was as rich as dark choco-late and every bit as sinful as those stolen swipes of frosting from her birthday cake. In spite of living in America for over a decade, his accent hadn't gone anywhere. He perused her from head to toe before those traveling eyes locked on her chest. "Christina. That's a pretty name."

Oh. Damn. Her badge! She'd clipped it on her top to make sure she would be admitted into the party but failed to tuck it away when she arrived.

Wait...

Reid knew she wasn't Christina, right? He had to be kidding. And so she laughed.

"Christina. Right."

"The tag's a bit of a formality but I'm glad for it. Saved me asking your name. I've been watching you dance."

Drew felt her smile slip. *Damn.* He didn't recog-nize her. A frisson of hurt rippled through her, and her smile was a little harder to hold. Was she so for-gettable?

"You noticed me," he said.

"What?" She blinked as she reframed the situa-tion in her head. She hadn't seen him in forever and she looked nothing like her former self. Still, she was halfway to offended that her brother's friend didn't know who she was...but she was also intrigued. What was the intrigue about?

Second chances, part of her whispered.

Reid knew Drew as Gage's little sis who was a fashion disaster, rarely spoke and was curled on the couch with a book whenever he had seen her. And though the summer she'd been rocking a black bikini at their family's backyard pool had been more about rebellion than catching Reid's attention, she remembered him noticing. In passing. He certainly hadn't looked at her the way he was looking at her now.

Like he *wanted* her.

What was that saying? That there wasn't a second chance to make a first impression. She'd bet there wasn't a single soul alive who didn't want to press a do-over button on something stupid they'd said or done in the past, to leave a totally different first impression. Evidently, she had the rare opportunity to do just that.

Reid and Drew both lived in Seattle—as did her brother—but she'd done her level best to keep from bumping into Reid on accident. Sure she'd undergone a transformation, but she wasn't willing to risk being overlooked again. He'd always seen Drew through the lens of "Gage's sister," and she doubted dropping weight and changing her hair color would change that. Not that she had to try hard to avoid him. Her social media footprint was almost invisible. She'd endured enough bullying in high school to know better than put up a photo and expect likes and wait for compliments. Nooooo thanks.

If she was running into him here, of all places, the universe must be nudging her to take action where he was concerned. It was a sign.

"Can I buy you a drink?" he asked.

A laugh bubbled from her throat. A second chance

to make a first impression on Reid. To find out how long it took him to realize that he was flirting and chatting with none other than *Drew Fleming*, Gage's younger sister, and not the mysterious "Christina" from the conference.

This should be fun. And no less than he deserved for not recognizing her on sight.

"Only if it's golden yellow and bubbly."

He eyed her gold shirt. "Fitting."

He offered his arm and she curled her fingers around his biceps. Whatever cool she had slipped from her like rainwater off a duck's back. She'd easily navigated the room in her high-heeled shoes all evening, but now worried she might stumble and fall. She swiped her teeth with her tongue in case her lipstick had transferred. She suddenly worried there was something in her nose or—

"Champagne and scotch rocks, please," Reid ordered from the bartender. Her palm was sweaty. So were her teeth, for that matter.

Do not freak out. Do not freak out!

She'd play a role. Like an actor. Deep inside she was the same Drew, but her outer appearance had changed enough that some days she felt like someone else. She was definitely a stronger version of herself. A *happier* version of herself. She'd sprouted and then bloomed, and now a tender new bud was around the corner. She could feel it.

Screw Chef Devin Briggs for never seeing the rose he'd had.

She shook her head. She wasn't going to let thoughts of her ex-boyfriend ruin a one-on-one with Reid.

"Golden and bubbly." Reid handed her the champagne flute. "Should we sit or linger?" He leaned in when he asked, and she was so focused on the shape of his upper lip, the tempting fullness of his lower lip, that she didn't answer.

"Huh?" *Smooth, Drew.*

He gestured to a cluster of boxy-looking chairs and a sofa in the corner. Currently unoccupied.

"Sit. Let's sit." Before she had a case of the vapors and fell flat on her face.

He took her free hand this time, his blunt fingers and wide palm dwarfing her smaller ones. She walked toward the sofa with one thought dominating all others. *I'm holding Reid's hand.* I'm holding Reid's hand!

She felt like a teenager again, smitten by this gorgeous god of a man who seemed too perfect to be real. Except she was closer to his equal now, wasn't she? The playing field hadn't been leveled, but close. She was a professional with a great job and a great life, and her shoes were adding four inches of much-needed height. She was confident and strong, and she wouldn't trade this second chance for anything. His being attracted to her was doing wonders for her ego.

Shallow, but no less true.

Dipping his chin, he gestured for her to sit. She did, crossing one leg over the other and noticing when Reid noticed. She hid her smile at the rim of the champagne flute. As bubbles tickled her throat and popped on her tongue, he settled in next to her.

"Where do you hail from, Christina—" another glance at her name tag "—Kolch?"

"And you pronounced it right. Impressive." Christina was always complaining that she'd heard everything from "Cock" to "Couch" whenever someone said her last name.

"Like the soda but with an *L*, I figured."

"You figured right." A weighty pause hovered in the air and she realized her faux pas. She recovered with a stilted, "What's your name?" and felt silly for asking.

"Singleton. Reid Singleton."

"Did you intentionally introduce yourself like James Bond, or did I hear it that way because of your accent?" His smile erased her mind like a powerful magnet, but thankfully she recovered quickly. "I assume you didn't grow up in California?"

"I'm from London, but I live in Seattle and have for years. Never developed a knack for you Americans' hard *R*s."

He overpronounced the *R* in *hard* and *R*s, which made him sound a little like a pirate. Drew laughed again.

"Do you always giggle this much or only when you drink champagne?"

"Only when I drink champagne with handsome strangers," she said, enjoying the game and the new rules for it. When Reid figured out who she was in the next two minutes, she would shove his arm in an ole-buddy-ole-pal way and chastise him for his weak powers of observation.

But she was in no hurry. She liked him this way— trying to win her attention, sitting taller when she'd paid him a compliment he had to know was true. It wasn't like Reid didn't own a mirror. He was obviously good-looking to the nth degree.

It was unfair to every other man on the planet.

"Well played." His voice was a low murmur as he leaned in, his eyes touching her lips. He then sat back, taking her breath with him, and sipped his scotch while she drained half her champagne.

She suddenly didn't want this to end. She didn't want him to recognize her. She wanted to be seen as charming and playful and beautiful. She wanted to relax and have fun and flirt.

Her gaze locked on his full lower lip below his contoured top lip. She wanted to kiss him. Before it was too late. Before she lost her nerve, and her only chance with it. As soon as he figured out that she was Drew Fleming, the moment would be lost.

A wave of panic sailed through her chest. She'd regret not kissing him for the rest of her life if she didn't do it now. She set aside her champagne glass and faced him.

"Tell me more about—" he started, but she cut him off. In the most delicious way possible.

She grabbed his dashing, perfect face, tugged his mouth to hers and kissed him hard.

Three

Reid's spicy cologne tickled her nose as she tasted his amazing mouth. She'd sort of slammed her lips into his to start—blame years of pent-up lust—but now she eased into a more tender kiss, sliding her lips over his in gentle exploration.

She didn't know if he felt the same electric sizzle that flamed to life inside her the moment their mouths met, but she accepted that this couldn't go on forever. When they pulled apart, she'd come clean. She'd tell him her name—her real one—and then she would do the awkward dance of apologizing for the subterfuge.

But when she would've ended the kiss, Reid's fingers fed into her hair, holding her close. He opened his mouth wide and stroked his tongue against hers.

That ignited flame inside her burst into a five-alarm fire. He kissed like no man she'd ever known. The slide of his tongue was ten times more intoxicating than the champagne she'd been drinking—*in and out, in and out*. A needy sound resonated from her throat.

Reid Singleton was even more delicious than she'd imagined. And, oh, had she imagined. In the darkest corner of her bedroom with a flashlight and her journal. A shoebox in her closet held some truly horrible poetry. She'd imagined him saying her name in his proper accent—not in polite greeting, but with passion.

She might never know what it was like to hear him say her name in that way, but at least she knew how he tasted. Like smoky scotch and sexy male. Every part of her from her peaking nipples to her overheating thighs wanted to climb onto his lap and satisfy the insistent throbbing between her legs.

His kiss was both thorough but careful, his skill and his tongue almost too much to bear. Here was a man who knew how to please a woman, and Drew was a woman who needed pleasing. *Badly*. Not just sex for sex's sake, but sex with Reid. Sex with the man who'd noticed her from across the room, who had always been polite and friendly to her and her family. The man who, if she told him who she was, would end this fantasy in an instant because he would never take advantage of his best friend's little sister.

She wanted to hover in the in-between forever. Where they knew each other physically, where the past had no weight on the present.

She palmed his chest, and even over a shirt, he felt better than he had in her fantasies. Hard and firm, and real. So real. Greedily, she ran her fingers to the open placket of his shirt and touched the bare skin of his neck. That's when he broke their connection.

Blinking like he was having an epiphany, he took her hand from his chest and held it, her fingers gripped lightly in his. She watched in horror as he studied her, his eyebrows drawn. She waited for recognition to hit, her own fear and worry a toxic mix. He'd recognize her, reject her—and possibly apologize for kissing her back, which would be worse than the other two combined.

Turned out he did that first.

"Apologies for that," he said, his accent thick, his voice tight with what she hoped was lust and not disappointment.

"Don't be sorry. I'm the one who kissed you." She licked her lips, needing another drink of her champagne like her next breath. She reached for the flute, but he beat her to it, handing over her glass. "I've wanted to do that for a long time."

A deep chuckle brought her eyes to his, and she held his gaze and silently asked the question she wouldn't dare ask aloud. *Did you figure out who I am yet?*

"All seven minutes you've known me, Christina?" His lips twisted temptingly. If that didn't answer her question soundly, nothing would. He still had no idea who she was.

She polished off the remainder of her bubbly. Disappointment had no place in the moments following kissing him, but it was there anyway, making her chest tight and causing her to feel something else. Sad, if she wasn't mistaken.

Beggars can't be choosers, Drew. You wanted to kiss him, and this was your only opportunity. Did you expect more?

More.

She blinked, the rogue thought so far from her good-girl tendencies she instinctively wanted to shut it out. Reid's throat moved as he swallowed a sip of scotch. His Adam's apple bobbed, and she chased the line of his neck to the scant bit of chest hair visible where his shirt gaped open—just below where she'd touched him seconds ago.

Lie or confess?

"I'm an impatient woman. That's why I kissed you." *Lie*, it was.

She wanted more. She wanted to run her tongue along his neck and kiss his bare chest. She wanted to kiss the firm, flat plane of his belly and trace that trail of hair down to the promised land. She wanted his mouth on hers, and lower. On her breasts and body, between her legs where she knew he'd be incredibly attentive and pleasing.

Although, if she walked out of this party without him—without telling him who she was—she'd be off the hook completely. She didn't hang around online and chat with old friends or new. She wouldn't cross Reid's path again unless Gage invited them to the same party—oh, shit.

Her brother's wedding!

Reid would *see Drew* at the wedding because he'd be there, obviously. Hell, he'd probably be the best man. He'd recognize her then, now wouldn't he?

That narrowed her options to an unfortunate one: confessing her real identity.

Reid tucked her hair behind her ear, then rested his arm over the back of the sofa. Leaning close, he watched her carefully. "I like impatience in a woman. And not to sound like a complete nutter, but I feel as if that kiss was inevitable. That even if you'd have waited seven more minutes, and seven more after that, it would've happened eventually."

Or maybe if I'd waited nine years. Ha ha ha...sigh.

He traced his finger along her jaw, his eyes following the path. Her heart rate was erratic. Could he see her pulse point thundering at the side of her neck? Then another, more devious, thought occurred. If she didn't tell him the truth just yet, how far could she take this night of fantasy? He'd forgive her. He'd have to. Gage and Reid weren't going to stop being friends because Drew told a white lie. Although one had to wonder if her own identity would be considered a "white" lie. Maybe off-white. Light gray...

"Like fate?" she whispered as he traced the scoop neckline of her shirt. This felt like fate to her.

"Bold word, but why not?" He continued touching her exposed skin, barely any pressure, the tickling sensation bringing forth goose bumps. "I also imagine that the evening will end with more than kissing if you'll allow it."

The skipped beat of her heart caused her breath to catch. "M-more?"

He trailed his hand to her palm and wove their fingers together. "A night together would amp up this conference to best-ever territory. I know you don't know me, Christina, but while I'm a man who enjoys a woman in my bed, I rarely mix work and play."

He lifted their entwined hands and kissed the top of hers, his stunning blue irises burning into her. She'd known Reid well enough to know that he didn't hold back in the physical affection department, but she'd never label him a player. That was too crass a word for him. He was simply a physical guy, acting on his instincts and his, she assumed, amazing skill. She couldn't imagine a single woman leaving his company being disappointed in his performance. Though many of them probably felt like she did: full of longing and worrying he wouldn't return her affections.

If ever there was a "seize the day" moment, this was it.

"What do you say? My room or yours? I'll let you choose, but mine is a suite with a kitchen, a balcony and a soaking tub."

"No piano?" She wanted to shout "yes!" but her nerves—or maybe her habit of always doing the right thing—had her stalling.

"No piano." His glorious chuckle might be the death of her. She wasn't a swooner, but she was close. "Room service and I are acquainted. I arrived two days before the conference started, and there wasn't an after-party with a beautiful woman in gold waiting to share my steak and movie."

"What movie?"

He grinned, maybe knowing she was stalling and not caring. *"Jaws."*

"Jaws!" His answer startled a laugh out of her. "How did you sleep?"

He let go of her hand, charm dialed to eleven as he swept his hand to her nape. He said one word— "fitfully"—before covering her lips with his and drinking her in for a kiss that lasted long enough to turn her brain to mush.

"Christina." His warm breath coasted over her lips.

Drew's eyes were closed, the pretending still in play. She could carry on this farce, let him seduce her for real and agree not to regret the sex. It wasn't as if she would've had a prayer of seducing Reid as herself, but as "Christina" she had a chance.

"Let me make your dreams come true," he said. "Come to my room."

It was everything she wanted to hear, but guilt niggled at her.

"Isn't that a secondary location?" she breathed. "I learned never to be moved to a secondary location."

Another light press of his lips, and she opened her eyes. It was like seeing him for the first time, that angled jaw, those entrancing eyes, the full mouth slightly pink from her recent attention. How could she say no?

She couldn't.

"That was a joke." She gripped his shirt and kissed him. He let her, which was thrilling. "I'd like to see your room, Reid. I'd like to see much more than your room."

Her heart was tapping out a salsa, her palms sweaty, her stomach a Tilt-A-Whirl of excitement. This was happening—really happening—and since Drew was a woman accustomed to setting goals and achieving them, she decided to stop justifying and embrace the moment. *This* moment.

"That might be the yes of my life, Christina."

She didn't know if he said that to all the girls, but she wanted to believe that it was just for her. They stood, leaving their glasses on the low table by the sofa, and then he led her away from the thumping bass of the speakers and out of the room.

Four

Drew entered the elevator and Reid stepped in behind her. The doors swished shut as he punched the button for the twenty-first floor.

She was in an elevator, alone with Reid Singleton, heading skyward to his hotel room, where they would have sex. Drew smothered a smile as she examined her strappy shoes, a flush of heat creeping along her neck as she imagined him removing those shoes and kissing his way up her calves…

She was as confident in his ability as she was in herself, although admittedly her confidence was fairly recent. Three years ago, at age twenty-four, she decided she'd no longer hide behind the excess weight or comfort herself by eating. She hired a personal trainer and cut out processed and fried foods and quickly dropped the unwanted pounds.

Drew loved food. Of that she'd had no doubt. But she didn't feel an ounce of shame admitting she loved food now that she had a healthy relationship with it. No longer did she soothe her negative emotions by eating; now she exercised or worked. She'd changed her mind-set—decided she was worthy of the good things life had to offer—and that had made all the difference.

A little over a year ago she'd achieved another goal. She'd been featured in *Restauranteurs,* an industry magazine, as one of the "Top 30 under 30" professionals. She'd been the only restaurant public relations manager in the magazine.

Her employer, Fig & Truffle, owned several restaurants, cafés and bars in and around Seattle. It'd been Drew's job these four years to oversee the soft openings. Seattle's foodie scene was massive. And after the feature in the magazine, Fig & Truffle boosted her pay and made Drew *the* PR go-to.

She handled press, booked reviewers, interviewed top chefs from around the world…which was how she'd met her previous boyfriend. Chef Devin Briggs was the cherry on top of her "I've arrived" sundae, but they didn't last. How could they when he was a selfish ass in love with only himself?

Jerk.

"Second thoughts?" Reid's smooth voice interrupted as the elevator bumped to a soft stop. He was watching her with curiosity and *not* in recognition, thank goodness.

"Not at all." She stepped out when the doors parted, pausing in the long corridor for him to lead the way. He palmed her lower back as they walked side by side, and again she became intently aware of him—of the breadth of his shoulders and warm weight of his hand on her body. Of his comforting presence.

There was an innate kindness to Reid one might overlook upon first meeting him. Probably because he was insanely gorgeous. That sharp jaw, full mouth and the hint of a dent at the center of his chin were so all-consuming it took a few minutes to realize he was human and not a futuristic sex toy designed solely for a woman's pleasure. Looking at him was a decadent treat—forget kissing him. Only she'd never, ever forget. Not even when she was ninety and gumming her food.

At the end of the corridor, Reid guided her to the right to a double-doored suite. He scanned his key, and gestured for her to go in ahead of him.

The suite was about one hundred times nicer than her room. She'd bunked at a hotel across the street from the convention center. Her room had a rattling air-conditioning unit, pilled, nubby carpet and wall hangings the color of pea soup. She'd have to tell Christina the next time her company offered to send her out of town to upgrade the room if possible.

Conversely, Reid's room was modern and posh. No piano, but the palette was a tasteful dove gray and pale ocean blue and minimally decorated with stylish furniture. The door opened to a wide sitting room with a couch and colorful throw pillows. A flat-screen television hung on the wall. A kitchenette and bar were on the opposite side, and the bedroom was visible through an open door across the room. Her eyes snagged on that room for a beat, imagining being laid on that stone-colored bedspread under Reid's blue-eyed attention…

Her recently earned confidence took a sudden dip.

"Nice. This is nice," she told him, her smile feeling brittle and forced.

"My company spoils me." He walked to a desk in the far corner, lifted the phone's receiver and murmured into it while she meandered around the suite. The bathroom was the size of her entire hotel room, the soaking tub wide enough for three people to sit comfortably.

"Champagne and strawberries are on their way up." She turned to see Reid stuff his hands in his pockets, his expression handsome and affable. "You didn't think I'd bring you up here and strip you bare right away, did you? Where's the fun in that?"

He untucked his hands and came to her, cradling her jaw. "If you change your mind at any time, Christina, say the word. I'm not owed anything."

"That won't happen," she whispered. "I need this more than you know."

A flicker of concern sparked in his eyes before a flame of desire crowded it out. She rested both hands on his chest, and he took the invitation to kiss her deeply. The only sounds were the soft suctioning of their mouths and the gentle scrape of the material of her shirt as he moved his palms over her arms.

Drew hadn't been with anyone since Chef Devin Briggs left her to start a family with another woman. Drew hadn't been ready for a family. She'd been building her career and enjoying her freedom. Devin, eleven years older than her, had already established his career and was ready to settle down. It'd been a frequent topic of argument between them, and had eventually led to their demise.

She'd been single since he left, working hard and skipping sleep in pursuit of becoming the very best at what she did. As a result, she hadn't had time to feel truly lonely. Christina had been there to distract her, chattering away about work or her own guy problems.

Drew had spent any free time she'd had researching and reading about food service and public relations, or staying up until the wee hours to call chefs in other countries who might be interested in lending their expertise to one of Fig & Truffle's franchises.

In short, she hadn't had the time or inclination to indulge her fantasies.

Until tonight.

Her fingers twitched with the urge to undo each button on Reid's shirt and kiss a trail over his hard chest to the muscular bumps of his abdomen. At the same time, she worried that somehow he would see her—the former *her*. That the pounds she'd lost would reappear in his mind and he'd recoil, leaving her feeling unworthy all over again.

Ridiculous, she scolded silently.

He nipped her bottom lip before peppering kisses on the side of her neck. Her worries dissipated with each press of his lips. Overcome by longing and the sensations in her sex-starved body, Drew gave in to the experience that was Reid.

He must've sensed that she was through talking or stalling, because next he bent and lifted her, propping her back against the wall. He continued kissing her neck and collarbone as she wrapped her legs around his waist. He anchored her there with his hips between her open thighs and—*oh!*

Her center lined up perfectly with the hard ridge of his erection, which made its presence known as it pressed against her most sensitive spot.

"Ready, both of us, then." He ground against her, sending her into a mental free fall.

She'd never imagined sex with him would be a reality. When she'd last seen him, she'd been eighteen and awkward and shy and quiet, and at that birthday party where she'd decided to wear the damn bikini, she hadn't missed Reid flirting shamelessly with the female bartender. While he'd ordered a beer, Drew had sipped on mocktails without a drop of alcohol. It'd been a good reminder of the gaps between them—not only the handful of years separating their ages but also of his class and stature. Of his sheer beauty and her averageness. Like a great sequoia next to a plain maple tree, anyone could see how different they were.

Tonight, she'd prove to herself she was worthy of the great Reid Singleton.

"I've been ready longer than you know," she said. His hair was thick and soft against her fingers. He smiled, his lips damp from kissing her. Once again she worried he was looking at her. *Really looking.*

She worried he might see that beyond her dark hair and curvy yet slimmer physique was the once-shy younger sister of Gage. She didn't want to become suddenly undesirable or untouchable.

So not an option.

Distracting him as best she knew how, Drew stroked Reid's crotch, pleased when the material of his pants tented invitingly. He groaned, his tongue plunging into her mouth as he took his sweet time.

She was ready—absolutely aching to have him inside her. He loosened his hold on her, and she untangled her legs from his waist to stand on her feet. She unbuckled his belt and worked his fly open as he tore his mouth from hers to suck in a breath. He freed her from her shirt and once her lacy pale pink bra was revealed, he froze, his attention on her breasts. They were generous and always had been, but appeared even bigger in the silky demicup bra she'd purchased to match her shoes. Her D cups were swollen and pressed together, her deep cleavage an invitation.

It was an invitation he eagerly accepted, cupping her breasts and lowering his face to kiss the tops of each one.

She'd worked hard on her body—keeping her waist trim and legs toned took a lot of work and effort. And since she'd worked hard, she was going to enjoy her reward. *Him*.

She unbuttoned his shirt as he slipped the bra straps off her shoulders, kissing her here and there as he did. She ran her hands over the expanse of his golden skin, and he tugged one bra cup down and sucked on her nipple. Her back arched, sending her breast deeper into his mouth, the resulting dampness in her panties a welcome warmth.

His mouth is the eighth wonder of the world, she thought, dazed by his skill.

He moved to her other nipple but before he could blow her mind, a sharp knock at the door preceded a call of "Room service!"

He lifted his face to hers, his eyes glazed with arousal. She fisted his hair in protest, and he winced in pain.

"Sorry," she muttered, letting him go.

"No, I'm sorry." He sent a baleful look in the direction of the door. She didn't want him to stop or even pause. She didn't want to give him a single moment to reconsider or change his mind. She couldn't bear the rejection.

He lifted her hand and kissed her palm before bending to retrieve her shirt and pressing it over her exposed breasts.

"Bedroom." His voice was rusty and sexy as hell. "I'll take care of this."

He crossed the room, his shirt and pants open, his hair a disaster.

Her grin was downright arrogant.

She'd weakened Reid Singleton's knees. What a powerful feeling that was. And he didn't seem anywhere near done with her yet.

At the door Reid buttoned his pants and ran his hands through his hair, sending her a wink as she backed into the shadows of the bedroom.

Five

Reid didn't bother closing his shirt or tidying himself much before letting the hotel employee in. He'd ordered champagne and strawberries, after all, which should've made it obvious that he was having a romantic interlude. He did tuck his hips behind the door when he opened it. What he was hiding from view would be too much information for whoever would wheel in the dessert cart.

A shaggy-haired guy who couldn't be more than twenty-one shuffled in looking bored and tired. Reid retrieved the first bill he saw from his wallet and stuffed it in the guy's palm.

Bloody hell. Reid had given him a fifty in his haste.

The kid held up the bill and blinked at it. "Wow. Thanks, man."

"No problem." Any amount of money was worth returning to his date as quickly as possible.

Door shut, Reid flipped the safety lock as Christina appeared from the dark bedroom. Her skirt was in place, those incredible shoes crisscrossing up her ankles. Her shirt was still missing—a good sign—and she was wearing a pale pink bra that barely encased her gorgeous breasts.

Those breasts might be the death of him, but what a way to go.

She repositioned the cups almost self-consciously as she walked toward him. He knew her breasts were both beautiful and delicious. He'd have to take more time admiring and tasting them. He also wanted to taste those thighs and higher. He'd had her legs around his hips, her molten center warming his straining erection. He needed her, and he needed her *now*.

"The cart's arrived." Not what he wanted to say, but he thinking was a challenge with all the blood flowing to his nethers.

"I see that." Her smile was so sweet that he couldn't shake the idea that he was taking advantage of her somehow. The way she'd said earlier that she'd been ready longer than he knew hinted that it'd been a while since she'd had a man in her bed. Likely longer since she'd had a man *who knew what he was doing* in her bed.

Through the women he'd known, he'd learned that men didn't make it their priority to pleasure a woman. Which was criminal. When gifted with a beauty like the one standing before him, how could Reid not take his time exploring every inch of that body to learn what turned her on? What made her moan or giggle? What made her gasp in surprise or go to the brink of where only he'd be able to take her...

Best not to rush if that was his goal.

He grabbed the champagne bottle by the neck and took it from the ice bucket. His date's smile slipped as her eyes went to his hands working the cork. Worry puckered her brow.

"Did you...change your mind?" she asked, and bless her breasts, she actually sounded serious.

A rough chuckle escaped him as he popped the cork from the bottle. "Definitely not. I'm attempting to be a gentleman."

"What if I don't want you to be a gentleman? What if I prefer hurried over slow?" She glided across the room like a petite runway model, skimming the couch with her fingertips, her shoulders back, those inviting breasts jiggling as she walked.

"Why? Have you somewhere else to be?" He filled the two flutes and nestled the champagne into the ice before lifting a silver dome to reveal rows of ripe red strawberries and a bowl of melted dark chocolate.

Her pink tongue touched the corner of her lips.

"A gentleman wouldn't rush to undress you right away. A gentleman—" he dunked one berry into the chocolate "—would sample the chocolate off your nipples while feeding you a strawberry."

She sucked in an anticipatory breath. He had her full attention.

"A gentleman—" he carried one of the flutes over to her "—would sip this from your belly button before kissing you where it matters most. Ever had an *effervescent* orgasm, Christina?"

The heat in her eyes banked. "I prefer *love*."

A request he'd heard before. Some American women liked that term, he assumed because of his accent. He wasn't below fulfilling their fantasies.

He approached with the strawberry, chocolate delicately balanced on the tip. He lowered it to her mouth while saying, "Ever had an effervescent orgasm, *love*?"

She took a bite of the chocolate-covered berry, her eyelids, coated in a shimmery gold shadow, sinking shut. She moaned, a soft "mmm" that turned him on far more than it ought to. With this woman it seemed the anticipation of what came next was as exciting as the act.

Fantastic.

He polished off the rest of the berry, tossed the stem aside and kissed her. She tasted of chocolate and sweet red fruit. When she looked up at him, her cheeks were flushed, her eyes begging for what he'd promised.

"You've been with the wrong men, *love*."

"Tell me about it."

He offered her the champagne, and she took a sip, licking her full, inviting lips, and his erection grew harder.

"We only have tonight, but that doesn't mean we

have to rush," he told her. "In fact, since we have so little time together it makes sense to savor it."

He thought of this as "the talk." He didn't want to spoil the evening with overexplaining, but he wouldn't go forward before setting the expectation. Where Reid was concerned, there was no possibility for a relationship. He had no desire to go down that road.

"Believe me, Reid," she said on a throaty laugh. "I didn't expect things to get this far." She touched the dip in his chin and wiggled her finger. "Tonight will have to be enough for both of us."

A ribbon of unease curled in his chest. Already he wanted more than tonight, and he hadn't even had her yet.

"Unless we change our minds," he heard himself say.

"Why would we do that?" She narrowed one eye, her mouth a tempting purse.

"Are you staying for the entire conference?"

"I am."

"What if you find yourself bored while you're here and crave my company?" He threw in a shrug like he wasn't anticipating her answer.

"Hmm. We'll see." With that noncommittal response, she put her palm on his chest and shoved him toward the couch. He was content to let her do as she pleased.

A side table lamp and the bathroom light glowed, but other than that the suite was dark. Even in shadow, Christina was inviting.

Despite the added height of her shoes, she had to stretch to kiss him. He held the flute out of reach and wrapped his arm around her waist, pulling her soft, supple curves against him and erasing every bit of his memory. He'd promised to do…something. With the berries, or was it the champagne…? She'd entranced him.

"We aren't rushing." That much he'd remembered.

"No. We're not." She stole the flute, drained the remainder of the champagne and set it aside. Then she pushed him onto the couch. "But we're not delaying, either."

She clicked off the lamp and straddled him, her breasts between them. He cupped his hands over her bra, rubbing his thumbs over her nipples until the hard nubs beaded beneath the fabric.

She gasped one word. *"Yes."*

"Does it hurt good, love?"

"So good," she agreed.

He unclasped the bra, freeing those bountiful orbs to the trusted homes of his palms. He took one nipple on his tongue and sucked hard, and she cried out—a sharp, high shout of pleasure.

When she wiggled her ass on his lap, his hips arched to find her—his cock eager to reach her warm, wet heat, his promises not to rush be damned.

Six

With his mouth on hers, it was easy for Drew to forget everything. Her past—*their* past—her insecurities, her stupid ex-boyfriend, her worries that Reid might recognize her…

Those yellow jacket-sized concerns had swarmed her mind earlier, but now they shrank to tiny fruit flies before vanishing in a puff of smoke.

Whenever he touched her, she was lost. Lost when he smoothed his hands up her legs, lost when he palmed her ass beneath her skirt and completely lost when his mouth teased her nipples once more.

"Yes, Reid." Damp heat pooled at the apex of her thighs as she moaned his name a second time. It was a plea. A plea for him to take her to physical release, to deliver her from the woman she'd been for the past year-plus. The overworked, sleep-deprived, slay-all-day boss she'd turned into… That woman was nowhere around when Reid Singleton kissed her. She was simply a woman—and for the moment, *his* woman.

He let loose her breast and propped his head on a bright yellow pillow. His elbows were locked, his hands wrapped around the spiked heels of her shoes. "You're beautiful."

The words struck like flint to stone. Words she'd always wanted to hear. She'd heard *cute* a lot growing up. She'd heard *pretty* once or twice. Hearing the word *beautiful* from him touched her in a deep, hidden place. He tugged her shoes gently by the heels and smiled. "Keep these on. These are what I first noticed about you. I'm afraid a fantasy brewed as a result."

Reid had a fantasy involving her and her shoes? How awesome was *that*?

"You wouldn't deny a desperate man his fantasy, would you, love?" He gave her his best puppy eyes.

She shook her head. She doubted he spent many, if any, nights lonely. He said all the right things. Looked the right way. Life's greatest pleasures must show up gift-wrapped on his doorstep.

Tonight, for example, she'd served herself up on a platter. And yet still he'd worked to seduce her. Not that there was any need. She'd been seduced by him years ago—the moment Gage stepped into their house for dinner and Reid walked in behind him. At the time she hadn't fully comprehended what that pinch in her gut was telling her. She'd stared, and when he'd waved hello in introduction, she'd hidden behind her hair and then run to her room. She hadn't had a single conversation alone with him, choosing to talk to her friends or her brother on the rare occasions she had seen Reid. Even on her eighteenth birthday, she'd climbed out of the swimming pool the moment he'd dived in. He was so out of her league, so unattainable, she hadn't even had the confidence to *converse* with him.

She noticed he'd been careful to mention that he didn't expect anything from her beyond what they shared physically. Probably he was used to delivering the bad news—that while he was glad to spend the night with a woman, he couldn't offer more.

But Drew had entered this situation knowing her time with Reid had an expiration date. Her eyes were wide open, her heart under firm direction to stay out of it. She was spending these precious moments with him to *carpe diem*, not because she expected forever. Besides, once he figured out who she was, this would be over faster than she could say the words "expiration date."

Lowering her lips to his for another kiss, she promised herself that after she made love with him tonight she'd tell him who she was in the morning. It wasn't right to continue to lie to him. Though she could forgive herself this indulgence, she thought as she opened the button and zipper of his pants. Telling him now would mean ruining everyone's fun. They might as well enjoy themselves.

"Your wish is my command." She offered her best saucy wink, raked her fingers over his bare chest and then scooted lower on his legs to pull down his boxer briefs. His erection sprang from the barrier, thick and inviting. "Oh God."

She hadn't meant to say that out loud, but it couldn't be helped. She'd never seen one quite this... *substantial*. Devin's was slightly above average—or what she'd come to think of as average. Reid's penis made others pale in comparison.

"Something the matter?" her cheeky Brit asked, his grin confident and sure.

"It's... You're beautiful. Everywhere I look. Every part I uncover." That was as honest as she'd ever been, but she wasn't going to do tonight halfway. She'd wanted Reid for so long there was only one way to be with him. *Completely.*

Before she'd gotten her fill of his nakedness, he sat up and pulled her to him. His arms banded at her back, pressing her breasts flat to his chest as he kissed the underside of her chin.

"No, *beautiful* is my word for you. *Beautiful* describes these breasts I can't get enough of." He rubbed his chest against hers. "*Beautiful* describes the way you fit up against me, and the perfectly mind-numbing way I'll notch into you as soon as I'm done tasting you."

"T-tasting me?" She blinked at him, speechless and excited for that possibility.

"Mmm-hmm." He dragged his tongue in a slow line from her jaw to her throat before kissing her pulse point. "I'm going to bring you to orgasm with my mouth, and then I'm going to enter you and bring you that way, too. We'll throw in a few more during and after if you like. But I'm starting with my mouth here." He cupped her center, the pressure from his fingers teasing her clitoris. "Depending on how well you react depends on how long I stay down there. But be forewarned, I am very good."

A giggle bubbled out of her, a result of nerves and shock, or maybe the cocky, confident way he spoke. "Are you now?"

"Try me. We'll find out together."

Without waiting for her to answer, he stood and lifted her, his hands molding her butt. She held on as he walked her to the bedroom. Being carried to a bedroom by Reid Singleton ticked another box on her sexy bucket list.

Not that he could ever be reduced to an item on a list, but...well...he sort of *could*. He was an experience. One she was going to enjoy.

He plopped her onto the bedspread and shucked his pants, socks and shoes. The curtains were open, the star-pocked sky throwing meager light into the room. Just enough to highlight the dips and bumps of his chest and abs. She stood by her "beautiful" declaration. He was a sight to behold.

Especially when he lowered to his knees, his forearms resting on the bed near her feet. He lifted and inspected one high heel, the fire in his eyes evident even in the darkened room. He parted her legs gently and, gripping each ankle, dragged her down the bedspread toward him. Her skirt rucked up around her thighs, the pooling material bunching at her back.

Reid's hands disappeared beneath her skirt, smoothing the skin of her thighs and then, finding her satiny matching panties, dragged them off.

"Much as I want to see these on..." He didn't finish his thought, tossing the garment over his shoulders and returning his hands to her thighs. Broad, warm hands. His fingers gripped her flesh, and admittedly there was more there than she preferred. Drew might have drastically changed her body, but she was far from perfect.

But this is my perfect, she reminded herself.

He was.

"It's too dark in here. I have to see you. I'm sorry." He moved to stand and Drew slapped her hands over his and pushed them high on her thighs again.

"No! I need you now. Besides, it's sexier in the dark." And she was so, so close to having him.

She needed to share this with him, and it didn't matter what he thought her name was—she was giving Reid the real Drew. He was experiencing her physically and emotionally. She'd never fake that.

"Please," she whispered.

"I can't resist that plea, love." He eased to his knees and with another rough tug, pulled her to the edge of the bed. Tossing her legs over his shoulders, he lowered his face to her center and dragged his tongue slowly over her.

With a gasp, she dropped her head to the bed, her fists bunching the bedspread helplessly as he repeated the motion. His tongue delved and teased, fast then slow. He'd barely touched her and already she was dissolving.

"Please." She gave herself over to the sensations of his flicking tongue and attentive hands. Those hands climbed her body as he continued devouring her, and when he gave her nipples a light pinch, she came on contact.

Writhing, twisting, she belatedly realized she still wore her pointed-heeled shoes. It took some restraint not to accidentally skewer him.

Before she caught her breath, he declared, "One," and then lowered his face again, doing his best to turn her into mush. She entered the veil willingly, giving herself over to him and coming again in record time. He didn't count aloud this time, didn't give her a chance to recover before he renewed his efforts and took her over the brink for number three.

Three orgasms.

Never in her life had she tumbled over back-to-back-to-*back*. His hands were resting on her breasts, and she pushed up on her elbows. The pleased smile on his face framed by her parted thighs wasn't a picture she'd soon forget.

"Don't brag," she huffed. "It's ungentlemanly."

They both laughed at that one.

He kissed the insides of each of her legs and then vanished from sight before returning again with a foil packet in his hand. He climbed over her body, every inch of him bare and beautiful. "I'd say you're more than ready for this part, love. Correct me if I'm wrong."

She did love when he called her "love." She'd originally made the request to keep him from calling her "Christina," but "love" was working for Drew just fine, thank you very much.

"You're not wrong." She tugged him to her and kissed him thoroughly, stroking his hard-as-steel member once, twice before moving her hand so he could roll the condom on.

"Skirt off," he commanded.

She lifted her hips and allowed him to slide the layers of material from her legs. "Shoes, too?"

"Never."

She smiled what was probably a big dopey smile, and he returned it with one of his own. Then he cocked his head to one side, his lips pursing like he might say something. Perhaps something like, "Drew Fleming, is that you?"

Fear rattled through her like a roller coaster on an unstable track.

You're so close. Don't give up now.

"I need you." She wrapped her ankles around his ass, crossed them and tugged. The moment his cock brushed against her, the blip of concern erased from his face like it'd never been there. He shifted, nestling closer as he kissed her thoroughly. In between the heady slide of his tongue on hers, he shifted his hips and slid home.

She pulled her lips from his to yell, "Yes!" but her

voice was no more than a strangled breath. A breath she lost when he slid out and then in again.

He fit, filling her, surrounding her. His scent, the rough, satisfied sounds coming from his throat—the entire experience of Reid—was better than she'd imagined. A growl rumbled in his chest as she smoothed her hands over his firm pectorals.

She'd never done this before—gone home with someone for one night. She never would've shared anything this intimate with someone she didn't know. She didn't know Reid that well, and yet there was something undeniably familiar about him.

"Ready for another?" he murmured against her lips. Their sweat-slicked bodies were smooth and damp against each other.

"Yes."

"Yes, what?" His smirk was too much.

"Yes…sir?"

"I was going for 'please,' but 'sir' will do." He tucked his arm beneath her knee and propped her calf on his shoulder. He drove deep, and that was the angle that sent her tumbling over for a fourth time. Before she could revel in the miracle of *Big O Number 4*, Reid gave in to his own hard-earned release. A guttural growl preceded a triumphant shout of completion.

She held on to him as the last of his orgasm shook his wide shoulders. He dropped his forehead to hers, panting out his release. When he let go of her leg, it drooped to the bed with the rest of her useless limbs. He gave her his weight, pressing her deeper into the bed, and resting his stubbled cheek on her shoulder. Satisfied and more than little sleepy, she tangled her fingers in his wavy hair.

She'd tell him the truth in the morning. After they both came down from cloud nine, or heaven, or wherever that last orgasm had taken her.

For now, she allowed her eyes to grow heavy. The radioactive hum in her body faded into a low buzz, and sleep's tendrils wrapped around her like a warm blanket. She became aware of Reid kissing her breast, her collarbone, her cheek. Of the bed shifting as he stood and shuffled into the bathroom.

The final words she recalled hearing were "Rest up, beautiful girl."

Seven

Reid listened to Christina's deep breaths in the dark, watched the rise and fall of the sheet he'd tucked her under, and smiled to himself. He'd been trying to fall asleep for a while. Four a.m. was an unholy hour to wake anyone. But as he brushed his fingers along her arm, the memory of touching her came crashing back, and parts of him refused to lie dormant.

They'd only just met and oddly enough, she felt familiar. It'd been a while since he'd connected—truly connected—with another person in bed. Sex was about satisfying a physical need, and yes, connection had happened before…on a purely physical level. With Christina, there was more than his body responding to her body. It was as if…his very *soul* responded to hers.

That was…that was…

Well, it was *insane* was what it was.

He blamed the hour, or maybe it was the lack of sleep. He couldn't possibly have a "soul" connection with someone he'd just met. It could've been due to the amazing sexual experience that had eclipsed any other from his past. He couldn't remember wanting anyone as badly as he'd wanted the woman lying next to him.

Not that it would change anything. Flynn's and Gage's recent betrothals weren't contagious. Reid had long beat the "I'm never marrying" drum, and now those drumbeats were more distant than ever. As much as turning over his heart as well as his bollocks scared him, thoughts of having a family sometimes intruded. Though that was definitely not in his best interest. Reid had lost his other half long ago, but still felt that loss as if it'd happened yesterday.

Physical connection was something Reid sought out and needed desperately, and tonight, when a beautiful stranger approached him, he hadn't had to think twice about throwing himself into an encounter with her. It was as simple as that. There was no sense in letting his past intrude in the present or in making this "connection" bigger than what it was:

Pure undiluted sexual attraction.

Christina hummed in her sleep and shifted, kicking the sheet off her body and baring her smooth back to him. She stuffed her hand beneath her pillow and revealed the side of her right breast and a splotch of color just behind it.

Familiarity prickled him. He had the strangest sense of having seen it before…

Then he realized he had.

Reid's brain skipped like a vinyl record. His eyes strained in the meager moonlight before he reached up to touch that spot, a distant memory warring with the present.

He traced the shape of the birthmark: the shape of the continent of Australia, and if he turned on the bedside lamp, he'd bet he'd see that it was grape jelly in color.

His body went cold as a flash of memory slapped itself onto the screen of his mind. Reid had gone at Gage's parents' house for a birthday party for his younger sister, Drew. She was turning eighteen, and Reid had brought a gift, though he had no memory of what it was now—and while he was flirting with the female bartender, Drew dropped her towel to reveal a black bikini. She'd scooped up her long blond—at the time—hair and tied it at the back of her head, clearly having embraced her curves enough to show them off at the privacy of her parents' pool. She'd lost the baby face—the rounder cheeks that she'd had when he'd met her. Reid had noticed the birthmark peeking over the string securing the barely-there top before she'd leaped into the water and avoided him the rest of the party.

He'd avoided her, as well.

There was no room for attraction to Drew. She was too young. Reid wasn't the boyfriend type. Plus, Gage's younger sister deserved only the best life had to offer—forever and a big diamond ring had always been in her future. They had never been in his.

Only now there was an attraction between them, wasn't there? It may or may not have been there at that birthday party years ago, but it sure as hell had burned between them tonight.

He snatched his hand away and scrambled out of bed, the mattress shaking as he did. Drew hummed once more but otherwise didn't move a muscle.

Hands fisted at his sides, he closed his eyes and prayed that when he opened them there'd be something in place of that splotch by her breast. An actual blob of grape jelly, or an illusion thanks to the shadows in the room.

No such luck. It was there in living color.

Drew Fleming was in his bed.

He swiped his forehead, irritated and angry in equal measures. She'd slimmed down since her eighteenth birthday. Her waist was nipped, though her breasts were large and ripe and her hips substantial. He should know—he'd touched, licked or kissed every luscious part of her tonight.

She was fit and strong, her hair no longer the blond with pink streaks he remembered but bold, sophisticated brown. And Drew herself was different. Even in that bikini that summer, she'd walked with her shoulders curled, her hair hiding her face.

It was the last time he'd seen her, so she hadn't been on his mind. Why would she? Other than the occasional mention Gage made of her, he'd had no interaction with her. He'd had no way of knowing the woman he'd taken to bed was Drew, especially when she'd introduced herself as *Christina*.

Reid's left eye twitched as he became aware of how naked he was—of how naked she was. He'd had sex—great sex—with a woman he couldn't easily disentangle himself from. It broke every rule he'd had for as long as he could remember.

Not to mention Gage would draw and quarter him if he ever found out Reid bedded his little sister with zero intention of a relationship.

Reid couldn't return to his life and she to hers like this had never happened. He'd shagged his best friend's sister while at a conference in California. He couldn't justify or rationalize that he was a male with needs and had thought she was a beautiful stranger with those same needs. Not now that he knew the woman in his bed was fucking *Drew Fleming*.

"Christ."

While Drew had undergone a radical physical transformation, Reid *hadn't*. He looked virtually the same. Sure, he'd gained muscle and mass, dressed more professionally. His hair was shorter than he'd worn it then. But aside from the lines around his eyes that hadn't been there in his twenties, he looked like himself. His hair hadn't fallen out, his belly hadn't grown fat and his accent hadn't changed, which meant Drew had known *exactly* who he was when she'd flounced over to him at that mixer.

He'd been so besotted by the beauty of the woman in gold, at the idea of charming her and getting her into his arms, that he'd overlooked that he *bloody knew her*.

She'd taken advantage of his single-mindedness, blinding him to her true identity. She'd allowed him to seduce her, to kiss her, to *go down on her*, all while knowing he had no idea who she was.

That not only made him feel completely daft, it pissed him off.

Was it an act of revenge? A plot against him? Had he done or said something to her in the past he didn't recall?

He pulled on his boxer briefs and rounded to her side of the bed, flicking on the bedside lamp. In the warm ambient light, Drew squeezed her eyes tighter in protest at the rude awakening.

She hadn't seen anything yet.

She reached for the sheet to cover her face, but Reid yanked it away, instantly regretting it. Her naked body was a beautiful sight and his cock, which didn't mind being misled, twitched in definitive interest.

Dammit. He concealed her beneath the sheet and snapped his fingers in front of her face.

Her eyes burst open, glazed and hazy with sleep before those sensual, full lips pulled into a crooked smile. She was gorgeous, but she was also a siren of the worst kind. She'd led him into the rocks. Tricked him. *Seduced* him.

She was gorgeous, all right.

A gorgeous *liar*.

Eight

Her night with Reid rolled over her like the tide sweeping the shore. It crashed into her with the ferocity of four—*count 'em, four!*—orgasms, and swept away memories of every lonely night spent bingeing sad movies and eating popcorn and feeling sorry for herself over stupid Chef Whatshisname. All that was left was Reid. Beautiful, charming, sexy Reid, who'd made love to her thoroughly…and was now waking her up abruptly.

She couldn't dredge up enough anger to take him to task for it, even though the bright bedside lamp was overkill.

"What time is it?" her morning voice croaked. She reopened one eye to focus on him, expecting to find his charming smirk or affable half smile. Instead, he was glowering at her from his full height.

"A bit after four."

Mmm. She could listen to him talk all day in that yummy British lilt.

"Drew."

"Why on earth are you waking me up at four? We don't have to report to the display floor until—"

Drew.

He'd called her Drew.

Shit on a shingle. He *knew*. Wide-awake now, she sat up, her earlier explanations and justifications sounding lame even to her sleep-clogged brain.

She was so stupid for believing that she could not only pull the wool over his eyes but knit him a complete sweater out of it. Dumb. Dumb, dumb, *dumb*.

"Listen, I can explain." She sat up and pushed her hair off her forehead, the sheet falling to her lap. He jerked the blanket up to cover her. Oh, right, she was naked. She clutched the blankets to her chest, guilt weighing her down.

"You said your name was Christina," he bit out through clenched teeth.

"Actually…I didn't say that. I wore Christina's name tag and you assumed—"

"You let me assume!" His voice was a thunderclap of anger, his hands righteously propped on his hips. "You never thought to mention you were my best friend's younger sister all grown up?"

"Don't lecture me, Singleton!" she snapped, the warm and cozy bliss from great sex and deep sleep now fully shaken off. "Was I so easily overlooked you had no idea who I was? Even as we had sex and talked and looked into each other's eyes?"

"You wanted to be called *love*." His tone was so lethal she winced.

"I know. I didn't want you shouting out Christina because it'd make me feel weird since she's my roommate."

A muscle in his jaw ticked, and she wished it would've made him the slightest bit less attractive so that she could stay angry with him. Sadly, it only made him look hotter.

He turned and walked out and her guilt tripled, even as she admired his sexy backside shifting this way and that in his black boxer briefs.

"Crap." She reached to the floor and found her panties and slipped them on. And since her gold shirt was about the least comfortable item of clothing on the planet, she rummaged through a drawer and grabbed one of Reid's white T-shirts. She pulled it over her head, unable to keep from lifting the soft cotton to her nose for a laundry-commercial worthy sniff. Then she ventured out to find him.

He stood at the window, stone silent, his back to the room.

"How'd you figure out who I was?" she asked, her voice small.

Reid didn't turn around. One deep breath lifted his wide shoulders, then one more before he finally answered her.

"Australia," he said. Strangely.

"Australia?"

"Your birthmark." He peeked over his shoulder at her, one eyebrow winging skyward. "Behind your breast."

Right. Her birthmark. "Oh. That."

"Yeah, *that*. Australia and grape jelly in color."

"I always thought of it as raspberry."

Shirtless, thick forearms arms crossed over his chest, Reid was imposing and inviting all at once. The bump in his boxers was at half-mast, large enough that her gaze snagged on it for a beat longer than appropriate.

"Drew."

"Sorry." She rerouted her eyes to find his expression less ragey than before. Then she thought about what she was saying and how she was acting. Shame-filled, apologetic, guilty. That was the old Drew.

Old Drew had since transformed her life, her body, her *very being* to become who she was today. She wasn't going to let Reid take that away from her. Not after they'd shared the most intimate act between them.

"No. You know what? I'm not sorry. You had no complaints about my name, or my breasts or the incredible sex we had a few hours ago. I'm not going to apologize for rocking your world."

His expression showed a dash of chagrin. *Good.*

"The truth is if you had known it was me, you never would've taken me to bed!"

"You're damn right."

Ouch. She'd expected that, but still didn't like hearing it.

"What did I do?"

She blinked, confused. "Huh?"

He took a step toward her, and then another until they were toe-to-toe and she had to incline her chin to look up at him. He asked that strange question again, enunciating each word. "What did I do?"

"I don't follow."

"To you? What did I do to you that you wanted to exact revenge on me? How did you know I was going to be here? Do you spy on Monarch Consulting? Did you ask Gage my whereabouts? This isn't going to end well when he finds out, Drew, you have to know that."

She let out an exhalation of disbelief and a laugh of pure derision followed. "Oh…my gosh. You think this was about you." His turn to look confused. "You self-centered—" She poked him in the chest to make her *literal* point.

"Hey."

"—egomaniacal—" *Poke.*

"Hey!"

"—selfish bastard!" A third poke in the center of his breastbone had him swatting her away, only he held on to her hand, refusing to let go. "You think I did this *to you*? You think I held some revenge fantasy in my head so that I could take advantage of you nine years later? Maybe you think I lost weight for you. Dyed my hair for you. Arranged for my roommate to have to flu so I could pretend to be her, *just to get to you*!"

She succeeded in freeing herself from his hold. She sniffled, angry that she'd let her emotions overcome her. Angrier that tears were building behind her eyes. Well, those tears would have to wait, because she wasn't done being pissed off at Reid "I'm Every Woman's Reason for Getting Up in the Morning" Singleton.

"You weren't a target, Reid. I did this for me. I used to have a crush on you so big it nearly took my knees out from under me. And the handful of times I saw you after, that bolt of attraction returned. But I was too young, or too overweight—"

"Drew—"

"Shut up, I'm not done." Unwaveringly, she held his gaze, daring him to interrupt. He pressed his lips into a firm line and let her finish. "I was too young, or too overweight, or too short to grab your attention back then. But not tonight." Her smile returned when she remembered him noticing her. "Tonight you were watching me. You said you noticed my shoes first. You bought me a drink and you flirted with me. And then you brought me here and—"

"I *know* what happened." He held up a palm to stay her words.

"Was it that bad for you? Because for me, it was…" Vulnerability was not her strong suit, but here she went. "It was really great."

He surprised her by tucking his hand under her

jaw and pegging her with a glare that rivaled the one he wore when he woke her up.

"How could you ask me that? You know how it was for me. You were there." His voice gentled.

"I knew you'd say no. That's why I didn't tell you my name. I had one chance for you to see me as someone other than Gage's little sister, and I took it." She shrugged. "I was going to tell you the truth in the morning. I thought I'd wake up before you did. I didn't know you'd knock me out with a four-pack of orgasms."

His rough laugh startled her as much as his fingers playing in her hair.

"I guess I didn't do as good a job of knocking you out since you were awake first," she said.

He dipped his chin, leveling her with an authoritative look. "I woke up ready to do it again. I was debating whether or not four a.m. was too early to wake you for another round."

Her "oh" was a startled puff of air. Round two sounded…wonderful. "Okay. I accept."

His headshake was subtle, but no less disappointing. But she could work with subtle.

"The conference lasts another four days. If we—"

"*No.* Are you aware that I see your brother each and every day at work? If he found out—"

"You think I'm anxious to tell Gage about who I'm sleeping with? I don't need his permission and neither do you. Unless you took some oath I'm not aware of not to date me I don't see the problem."

There it was. That smirk she found stupidly attractive. And since he'd given her an inch, she continued her side of the argument.

"I know you're not looking for anything permanent—trust me, after my last boyfriend, neither am I." She rested a hand on Reid's naked chest.

"Drew." He put his hand over hers. "We can't."

"Why not? Do you regret it?" A second passed. Two. Three. *Four.* "Tell me why we can't take off the clothes we're wearing right now and have sex like we did earlier. Tell me why we can't, and I promise I'll get dressed, leave and I won't bother you for the rest of the conference. Or ever again."

Part of her screamed in protest, but she wouldn't accept pity sex, especially from Reid. If he regretted sleeping with her that much, they'd be better off chalking last night up as a onetime thing. She'd have the memory of the best sex ever, and that would be enough.

That would *have to* be enough.

Nine

How could he look into Drew's warm coffee-brown eyes and lie? He couldn't. Even though he should. He should tell her that having sex with her was a mistake not to be repeated, and that while she didn't have to avoid him entirely, any physical endeavors between them were well and truly off.

He should tell her the reason *why* was because he wasn't a good guy for her to waste her time with. He should tell her that Gage was too good a friend to lie to, even by omission.

He *should*.

She was delicate swimming in his white T-shirt that covered her panties and hung low on her arms. Her eyes turned up to him in open vulnerability, and *dammit*, he couldn't lie to her. She siphoned the truth out of him like a needle in a vein.

"I don't have a good reason why," he admitted. "And no, I don't regret it. I was surprised when I saw that birthmark. I didn't recognize you last night, which made me feel daft. I should throw you out on principle alone," he added sternly.

She tucked her chin and batted her lashes, peering up at him with wide, doe-like eyes. That made her look like a naughty schoolgirl he'd like to take over his knee. It'd be no less than she deserved.

"But if I threw you out," he told her, gripping her nape, "I'd never again have the chance to do this—" He kissed her, sliding his tongue along hers and tasting that familiar-but-not flavor he'd become acquainted with. "And I want to do that again, Drew." He studied her carefully. "Or do you prefer to be called 'love'?"

"I prefer Drew." Her cheeks grew pink, lust darkening her widening pupils.

He lifted the hem of the T-shirt she wore and tossed it aside, taking a moment to admire those lush breasts begging for his tongue. He gave in to their plea, kissing the rosy buds as she moaned in his ear and tickled his scalp.

Hand between her legs, he pressed his fingers against her silky panties to find her damp and ready for him. "That didn't take long."

A sharp yank drew his head back, and he was facing Drew Fleming's wrath, her eyes twin pools of dark chocolate, her pursed, full lips determined. "You still have to work for it."

"Do I?" He loved teasing her. He'd enjoyed it last night, and he found himself looking even more forward to it in spite of knowing her true identity. She wasn't a one-night stand; she was someone he knew. Someone he shouldn't be with. *Forbidden.*

As much as he desired connection and release for himself, he craved her release even more. Craved those heady sounds of satisfaction as he gave her exactly what she wanted. Craved hearing his name roll off her lips, and saying her name as he lost himself inside her.

Her *real* name.

Propelling her backward, he walked her to the nearest wall and pressed her against it.

"Oh, back where we started," she said playfully.

"Yes, except this time we're doing everything against this wall. Later, if you like, we can have another round on that chair." He tipped his head to gesture to the chair sitting adjacent to the sofa. "And then over there on that kitchenette counter, or maybe the bathroom counter."

A flare of excitement widened her eyes.

"Bathroom counter, then?"

"What?" She blinked like she hadn't expected him to say that.

"You seemed excited by the prospect of the bathroom counter." He quickly carried her to the bathroom, plopping her onto the smooth marble surface.

Only one sink, so the length of the counter was wide open for other endeavors. "I'm here to serve."

He smoothed his fingers from her neck to the valley between her breasts, purposely avoiding touching her exposed nipples. "Why did you like the idea of the bathroom, Drew?"

He suspected why, but he wanted to hear her say it. By everything she'd told him he could guess that she'd had a few fantasies that hadn't been sufficiently exceeded. He meant to change that.

"Um." Those cheeks went pink again before a nervous laugh parted her beautiful mouth. Just when he thought he'd have to tickle the answer out of her, she said, "Because of the mirror."

"You'd like to look in the mirror during?"

"Don't sound so shocked. Look at you. Like I wouldn't want to watch while we're...you know."

Could she be more darling? With all that dark hair coasting over her shoulders and her eye makeup slightly smudged, she was girl-next-door sexy with a million curves he wanted to road test at every possible speed. Breakneck, stop-and-go, snail's-pace slow...

"That's where you've got it wrong. You're the one to look at in that scenario." He slipped off her panties and discarded his boxers, helping her off the counter. He turned her to face the mirror. The lighting was bright and revealing, and the more he saw, the more he wanted. "Is it any wonder I was too gobsmacked to recognize who you were? Look at you."

He smoothed her narrow shoulders with his palms,

slid over her biceps and took her hands in his. He held her arms to her side, and watched as her breasts lifted, the perfect quarter-sized nipples puckering in the cool air streaming in from the AC vent. From there he traced his hands along her ribs until she giggled and clasped his hands in hers.

"I wondered if I'd have to tickle that answer out of you earlier, and here you are, *ticklish*."

"Don't use that against me, okay?"

"Never," he lied, kissing her cheek as he clasped both her wrists behind her. "Now, where were we?"

He smoothed his hands over her belly, and she winced. "Not there."

"Why not? I like this part." Her belly wasn't completely flat, which he adored. Her curves were what he'd found most attractive. "I like how you feel against me."

He cupped her between her legs, gentling her open and swiping a finger along her seam. Kissing her ear, he watched her in the mirror. Her eyes were closed, her breasts heaving with her breaths, her mouth open in a pre-orgasmic O.

Bloody gorgeous—he was a lucky bastard.

He continued stroking and talking while she dissolved against him.

"I like all your soft bits against me. The soft and the hard make for great contrasts." He let go of her wrists and bumped her full bottom with his erection. She moaned her approval.

With one hand he increased the slick friction between her legs while toying with her nipple with the other. Then he offered a quick bite to her earlobe and breathed into her ear, "Drew. Open your eyes."

She obeyed Reid's command, and her gaze clashed with his in the mirror. She was surrounded by his tanned, broad form and thick shoulders. His fingers, dark against her pale skin, moved between her legs, and with each upward stroke she had to resist standing on her toes. She didn't know if she wanted more pressure or less. If she should ease away from the sensation or lean into it. He was too fantastic—too beautiful. Too…everything.

"My God, look at you."

He kept saying that, and as much as she wanted to stare at his perfect beauty, she obeyed his command and looked at herself. At her flushed face and neck, at the rosy nipples, one of which was being plucked lazily by the man behind her. At her hips and belly she'd never quite been able to rid herself of, damn her love of bread.

"You're perfect," he whispered.

"I've already agreed to sleep with you. You don't have to seduce me." She released a nervous laugh.

Reid straightened behind her, taking his tantalizing touch with him when he went. His face was an unreadable mask.

"What happened?"

"You think I'm lying?"

"Not exactly. I think you're being nice, and I was letting you know you don't have to be." She gave him a brittle smile. He took one final look at her and left the room. Left!

Before she could follow him out, he returned, condom in hand. He tore the packet open with his teeth, sheathed himself and returned his gaze to the mirror. She was forced to regard their reflections to meet eyes with him.

"I—"

"Do you want to have sex with me, Drew?"

"Of course."

"Do you want to have sex with me in front of this mirror… *Drew*?"

"Yes."

"While we have sex in front of this mirror, I will tell you how beautiful every part of you is while we do it, is that understood?"

His commanding tone excited her as much as the promise. She'd never been great at admitting she was beautiful or desirable. She'd never been that great at sex with the lights on. But she wanted to be different and she wanted Reid, and what he was offering was bold and inviting. It was exactly what she craved. Her entire body vibrated with *yes* at his offer.

"Understood."

"You have the most beautiful ass." He grabbed a handful of her butt, and she stood to her toes. At the same time, he bent his knees, lining himself up with her slick center. "Say yes, Drew."

She gave him a sweet smile in the mirror. "Yes, Drew."

"Cheeky." He notched into her, and she gasped

in anticipation. She didn't have to wait long to feel the rest of him. He slid in deep, each rocking motion slow and intentional, and the entire time he praised a different part of her body that he liked.

He held her chin and kept his gaze on hers, his voice turning her on and filling a deep cavern she hadn't known existed until just now.

This time with Reid was bold. It was different. It was *amazing*. And when he came, it was her name— *her real name*—that fell from his lips on a harsh growl.

Ten

"The Bachelor *What*?" Drew rolled and faced him in bed, the sheet slipping down revealing those luscious breasts, and everything Reid had been saying flew right from his head.

One finger on his jaw, she turned his head to hers meaningfully. "You really are a boob guy."

"I happen to like breasts, yes, and yours happen to be a very fine pair." Unable to help himself, he cradled one and tested its weight, brushing his thumb over the nipple for the sheer joy of watching it pebble in reaction. "They're magical."

"Uh-huh. Anyway. The bachelor thing…"

"Pact. The Bachelor Pact. Gage, Flynn and I agreed never to marry, swore on our—" He thought of what they'd sworn on and decided against sharing. Swearing on their dicks sounded immature at best and sadistic at worst. "We swore an oath not to abandon the others. And then they all abandoned me and left me the only man standing. Wankers."

"I love that word." She grinned. "I can't believe Gage is engaged…again. I didn't know about the pact, but it doesn't surprise me that he entered into such an agreement. I never thought he'd marry after the way his ex left him.

"We all have our sad stories."

She hummed in her throat, her eyes darting away. She'd hinted at her own sad story earlier but now didn't feel like the time to bring it up. His eyes slid to the alarm clock on the nightstand. The symposium opened at 9:30 a.m., and it was half past six now. Closer and closer to the time for them to pack up and hustle to work for the day.

"When do you need to go back to your floor?"

"My *floor*? I only wish I were staying at this glam hotel. I'm in the terra-cotta-colored flophouse across the street. It has three floors and the elevator is busted. My roommate evidently has a cheap boss. Unlike you."

He didn't like hearing that she had to schlep across the street and then back again. "I'll walk you over."

"Don't be ridiculous." With the tip of her finger, she *booped* his nose like she might a kitten's. "But that's sweet, thanks."

He snatched up her hand. "I wasn't being sweet. I was being protective, and it wasn't a question. *I'll walk you over.*"

He could've done without the eye roll.

"Fine."

He took advantage of her nearness to press a kiss to her lips. She lingered and he let her, and when they pulled apart he grunted in protest.

"I don't have that much time, Romeo. I can pull myself together fast, but not fast enough for another hour-long *sex*travaganza."

He enjoyed listening to her talk. The words she used, the unabashed way she complimented him.

"*Fine*. We'll talk instead. Tell me about your job. Your real job when you're not moonlighting as your roommate." He raised an eyebrow, and she beamed at him. Gorgeous girl.

"I'm the go-to public relations guru for Fig & Truffle restaurants. They have several local Seattle chains, and I'm in charge of running their soft openings, interviewing chefs to design their menus and a bunch of other stuff you'd find boring."

He didn't find her boring. He found her fascinating. "What's involved in a soft opening?"

"Well, it's when the restaurant is staffed, the menus finalized, the kitchen staff hired. Everyone is green and not quite ready for prime time. They hold a soft opening for friends and family so that the staff can practice, and then sometimes they'll do one for industry, like food critics. After that, the restaurant will open to the public, hopefully with a long line wrapped around the block."

"And you bustle around making sure everything is in place?"

"Pretty much. But it always is. I'm incredibly organized and meticulous."

He could envision her now, dressed in a sleek black dress, that dark hair pinned up in a fancy twist, her high-heeled shoes in place, her jewelry and makeup just so. In charge and confident in her abilities. A confidence that was newly won. From what he remembered of Drew when she was younger, she'd mostly hid her face from him.

"You're thinking something you're afraid will be rude to say." She squinted at him. "I can tell."

"I'm not."

"You are. Go on. Ask."

"It's not a question, more an observation. You've changed is all."

"Yes. I lost a lot of weight."

"That's not what I was thinking about."

Genuine surprise colored her features. "Really?"

"Really. I was remembering how shy you used to be, and now you're this bold, beautiful, confident creature who clearly gets what she wants when she wants it." He gestured to himself. "Look at me. I said we were done, and you've convinced me otherwise."

"It didn't take much convincing."

He kissed the smile off her lips and stole a glance at the clock. "I think we can fit in one more round and still have you ready in time. Especially with a capable escort chaperoning you to your hotel and back again."

Her eyes sparkled, a thousand yeses twinkling in their depths.

He parted her legs and climbed over her, staring down at Drew Fleming. How had he never looked this closely at her? Granted, he'd only seen her a handful of times, but how had he overlooked her slightly crooked smile, her infectious laugh, the alluring way she said his name…

"I should've known it was you," he told her.

"It's okay. I'm different."

"Yes, but I don't recall how you were before, short of a few sparse details. I should've paid more attention."

She twined her fingers into his hair. "Hmm. How could you possibly make it up to me?"

"I don't know that I can." He kissed one breast and then the other. "But I'm damn sure going to try."

Drew had spent so long in bed with Reid this morning, they'd been late to the symposium. He'd dropped her off at her booth, handing over the leather bag that he'd insisted on carrying for her. Then he'd kissed her sweetly before jogging to his own booth.

She'd set up with a smile on her face and her head in the clouds. She still couldn't believe that she'd spent the night with Reid Singleton, or that she was going to spend another night with him. He'd told her in her room—after agreeing that it was as subpar as she'd described—that he'd like to see her again tonight. She should've played coy or hard to get, but she'd blurted "Absolutely!" before she'd thought better of it.

The hours passed slowly, the crowds slower than yesterday. That gave her time to daydream, and she had plenty of fantasy fodder after what she'd spent the night and this morning doing with Reid. About fifteen minutes before she could close her booth, Drew began putting small things away to save herself time, like business cards and plush squishy balls with Christina's company's name on them. Her phone vibrated on the counter as she bent to toss the squishies into a cabinet.

"Hello, Christina," she said with a smile as she put the phone to her ear.

"Hello, Christina Two," her roommate said.

"You sound better. Out of the woods?"

"Eh. I managed to shower and heat a can of soup, but my energy level isn't great. Couch and TV are the only activities on my agenda."

"If that what it takes to get better, do it!"

"Are you ready to choke me yet for sending you to the symposium in my stead?" Christina let out a rattling cough, and Drew bristled in sympathy.

"Of course not. Plus you didn't *send* me, I practically begged to come." She debated for a full half a second before deciding to broach the topic of Reid. Christina didn't know him, and Drew needed someone to talk to. "I ran into someone I knew from a long time ago, so it hasn't been that bad."

Ha! Understatement of the millennium. Not only was her evening "not bad" it was so good it needed its own category.

"Anyone I know?"

"No. Friend of my brother's. His name's Reid."

"Whoa." Christina's cough sounded distant, like she'd held the phone away from her face. "Sorry about that," she groaned, and then sniffed. "As I was saying before my case of tuberculosis rudely interrupted: *whoa*."

She loved her friend's sense of humor. "'Whoa' what?"

"Your voice went all breathy when you said 'Reid,' only I can't do it because I sound like Stevie Nicks right now. Let's hear it. What happened?"

"Well, he…he thought I was you."

Silence.

"I don't mean that he thought I was *you* you. He didn't recognize me at the mixer and kept calling me 'Christina.'" She recapped Reid's flirting with her and how she hadn't corrected him when he assumed she was someone else. "And then I sort of… kissed him and agreed to go to his room. Which is a hell of a lot nicer than yours, by the way. You tell your boss the next time—"

"Drew Marie Fleming!" Christina exclaimed, probably using the last of her energy reserves. "You saucy tart!"

Drew shushed her friend and drew a curious glance from her booth neighbor across the aisle.

"Did he figure out your true identity?"

"Yes. He did. Sadly, before I told him. I was asleep…after, and he recognized my birthmark."

"Ah, rookie move, Fleming. You should've hidden that with makeup before taking him up to his room to blow his mind. Oh my God! I'm still in shock. Tell me everything. How was he? Are you seeing him again? How mad was he, or is he still mad?"

"I'd love to linger, but I'm about to close the booth for the day and I promised I'd meet him for dinner."

"That answers that. Oh, honey. You owe me so many details. And I owe you for going for me. Name it. Want me to cover your half of the rent this month?"

"You don't owe me. As good as last night was, and as promising as tonight is, I'm the one who owes you."

"That makes me happy." Christina's smile could be felt through the phone. "You deserve good things, Drew."

Drew teared up a little at that. She did deserve good things. And Reid was a very, very good thing. "Talk later, babe. Get well."

"Bye, hon."

She pocketed her cell phone and made quick work of clearing out the booth. After an arduously long day of boring tech talk, Drew was ready for a cocktail. She locked the expensive projector and other technological wonders for her display into the cabinet. Then she headed into the melee of hardworking men and women who had staffed their company's booths, and who all looked equally ready for a cocktail.

She found a sign in the aisle with a map of company names and booth numbers. Monarch Consulting, both three-zero-three, was one aisle over from where she stood now. She wandered past booths that were either empty or quickly emptying, and spotted Reid bent over a counter chatting with a prospective client...

At least she hoped the lithe, leggy redhead talking to him was a prospective client.

Eleven

Drew ducked behind a plant to watch Reid laugh and charm the redheaded woman. Even from the back she seemed pretty, in a well-fitting pair of pants and a shirt. And she was tall, which was something Drew would never be no matter how much she worked out.

She self-consciously smoothed a hand over her floral skirt. She'd paired the slim skirt with a bright pink top and gold jewelry, her heels gold and glittery. Reid had commented on how she liked to sparkle when she'd slipped them on. He'd been sitting on her ugly olive-green-and-pink bedspread in her room and she'd remarked how he looked good in everything— even the hotel's putrid decor.

And now that dazzling smile and his full attention were turned on another woman.

Memories of being with Chef Devin Briggs crashed onto her like a stack of toppling boxes. When he'd pitched the idea of them traveling the world together, she'd been intrigued, but also wary. She loved her job and living close to her family and wasn't ready to give either one up. Heck, she had her job to thank for meeting Devin—who'd she'd called to design the menu for Parity, a swanky café downtown.

She'd told him she wasn't ready. He told her he should've known better than to date someone "so immature" who didn't take life "seriously."

They broke up that night, and his infamous chef's temper she'd seen many times in the test kitchen made its final appearance. Only two weeks passed before he found Drew's replacement. Last she'd heard Devin and his new wife were opening a restaurant in France.

Even though Drew knew Devin was a selfish ass and turning him down had been the right call, getting dumped stung. When she'd heard he was "in love" via mutual friends at work, she'd felt replaceable and worthless.

As she watched Reid flirt with a woman the way he'd flirted with Drew last night, jealousy blazed brighter than ever. She stepped out from behind the decorative plant, determined to tell him exactly where he could shove that thousand-watt smile.

Screw this. Screw *him*.

Reid spotted her and straightened from his lean, his smile fading. The slender woman—in a pressed pair of black slacks and a blue silk shirt—turned, her smile catching, as well.

Drew stopped dead in her tracks, blinking in shock at the redhead. "Andy?"

"Drew!" Andrea Payne jogged over and scooped Drew into a hug. Andy was Gage's fiancée, Drew's future sister-in-law. She could kick herself for not recognizing the other woman's unique shade of strawberry blond.

"I'm so relieved that it's you. I thought…" Drew flashed a glance at a bemused Reid before pasting a smile on her face for Andy. "Never mind what I thought. What are you doing here?"

"I was hired to help a company across the street, and I saw the symposium signs. I thought I'd come say hi to Reid. Gage didn't mention you were going to be here." She frowned in confusion. "If I'd known I would've taken you to lunch."

"Thanks a lot." Reid folded his arms over his chest. "You barely fit me in five seconds before closing time, but Drew you'd treat to lunch."

"I like her more than I like you." Andy smiled sweetly at Reid, then turned to Drew. "So? What gives?"

"My roommate has the flu, and I offered to stand in for her." Drew pointed at her name badge that read "Christina" before removing it and tucking it into her purse.

"Did you know she was here?" Andy asked Reid.

"I saw her at a mixer last night. We, um…chatted."

"Reid and I haven't seen each other for years. He

didn't recognize me." Drew liked having sharing a secret with Reid, but Andy's being here made playing with fire feel more like playing with a live grenade.

So much for her brother not finding out Drew was in California at the same time as Reid.

"I wish I could take you both to dinner, but I have to get back to my client. What a fun coincidence." Andy cocked her head at Drew. "Where's your booth?"

"One aisle and three booths over." Drew pointed to the general direction of where she'd spent the day.

"What are you doing in this aisle? Did you two have plans or something?"

"Yes," Reid said. "I offered to buy Drew dinner in retribution for not recognizing her, so that's where we're headed."

"That was…thoughtful." Andy's blue eyes broadcast her suspicion, but then she blinked and it vanished like it'd never been there. "Well, I should go. Drew, great seeing you."

"You, too."

Andy whisked away, and Reid slipped his laptop into his bag, whistling as he locked up his booth with quick efficiency.

"Do you think she figured us out?" Drew murmured, eyes glued to the aisle where Andy had vanished.

"Do I think she saw us here, outside the Monarch booth, and assumed we spent the night in various stages of nakedness interspersed with champagne and bathroom counter sex? No. I do not think she figured us out."

Drew opened her mouth to tell him his smart-ass comments weren't appreciated, but he grabbed her and kissed her soundly before she could. She fisted his button-down shirt to shove him away but then ended up pulling him in as she enjoyed the firm feel of his lips on hers.

Mmm. He was addicting.

He ended the kiss and dropped another brief peck on the center of her mouth. "Now, if I'd done *that*, I do think she'd have suspected something. Also, what'd you mean when you told her you were relieved it was her? Who did you think I was talking with?"

"No one."

"Drew."

"I like when you say my name in ecstasy, but not in that scolding tone."

He reminded silent. *Waiting.*

Dammit.

"My ex didn't waste any time hooking up with someone else after our breakup, okay?" She lifted her arms and dropped them at her sides again.

"No. It's not okay."

"You're right. It's not. After that, I spent a lot of time believing I'm replaceable. I guess seeing you turn your flirt-o-meter up to eleven made me a little… concerned."

His eyebrows rose. "You mean jealous."

"*Concerned.* For myself."

"Mmm-hmm."

"Take that smirk off your face, Singleton, or I'll remove it for you."

"Promises, promises." He nuzzled her nose with his, the scent of his cologne tickling her senses and doing a good job of making her forget why she was upset.

"Did you decide on what to have for dinner?" He released her, and she missed being in his arms instantly.

That wasn't good.

She'd have to figure out how to have a casual affair since she'd never had one before. The trick would be walking away without developing feelings for Reid. And now, thanks to Andy's surprise visit, she'd also have to practice not looking as guilty when her brother inevitably brought up her running into Reid.

"Italian? Indian? Burgers and fries?" The man occupying her thoughts ducked into view, and she realized she'd spaced out for a second.

"Wherever is fine."

He shook his head. "You're a foodie. 'Wherever' is not fine."

Okay, he had a point. She wasn't sure it was a good idea to go to dinner with him, especially since she knew she'd end up in his bed afterward. But he was so...*yummy*. Plus she liked that he was standing there waiting for her answer, like what she said would alter the course of his evening. That kind of power was heady.

"Masala is good, and it's four blocks from here.

We can walk. I need to drop off my stuff at my room first. Meet you there?"

"Meet me there? Good God, woman, who besides that asshole chef have you been dating? I'll take your things up to my room. We can walk together." He gestured for her leather bag. "I was thinking about how inconveniently located your room is from here. Why not stay with me for the remainder of the conference?"

"Wh-what?"

"You heard me. I have plans for us. You're not going to be in your room anyway. Just check out on Sunday and Christina's boss will be none the wiser. We've agreed to spend these days together, so might as well spend them *together*."

Everything sounded so good when he said it. Even—*gulp*—what translated loosely into moving in together. A little prickle of concern tickled the back of her mind, but she shoved it away. Staying in the same hotel room with Reid wasn't the same as embarking on a yearlong relationship destined to end in disaster. When Sunday came, they'd return to their separate lives in the same big city and everything would go back to the way it was before they slept together. She'd see to it.

Just because she'd had a Devin Briggs flashback a few minutes ago was no reason not to have fun with Reid. Besides, they were nothing alike. Reid didn't have OCD, wasn't temper-prone and didn't order her around. She didn't count his insisting on walking her to her hotel, or the sexy, commanding tone he'd used when they were having sex in front of the mirror. That was more about him taking care of her needs than throwing his weight around.

"Masala it is," Reid said. "I'll run your bag upstairs."

"I'll come with you."

"Oh, you will, will you?"

"I'd like to move my legs. Other than fetching a sandwich from the food cart, I haven't had a chance to raise my heart rate."

"Love, I can think of many more fun ways to raise your heart rate." He sent her a foxy wink, shouldering her bag as they walked to the elevators.

He wasn't wrong. That wink alone had elevated her heart rate better than power walking or taking the stairs.

"But you can't seduce me yet," he told her as they stepped into the elevator. "I deserve a nice night out, I've been stuck in my room since I arrived. I won't let you keep me there like some kind of sex slave."

"Me?" she asked as the doors swished shut. "You were the one who was all 'my room or yours.'"

"First, I do not sound like that."

He didn't. Her British accent was rubbish.

"Second, I want to talk. We've a lot of history to catch up, you and me." He winked again. So sexy.

"What if Andy sees us?" she asked, her concern returning.

"It's a big city. Plus I wasn't planning on shagging on the table when we went out."

She snorted.

"Do you always snort when you laugh?" He smiled at her, and she realized that she really liked when he smiled at her. There was something possessive behind it, and yet that possession didn't make her feel smothered.

"That was embarrassing, and you pointed it out."

"It was embarrassing? I thought it was cute."

"*Cute.* I hate that word."

The doors opened, and he held them for her to step out. "Why?"

"It's nothing." In the corridor, she turned the direction of his suite.

"Might as well tell me. I'll find out for sure now that I know you're ticklish." He swiped his key card and opened his hotel room door to reveal a room tidier than they'd left it. The maid must've been in. Reid dumped his bag and hers onto the couch.

"Why do you hate the word *cute*?"

She shrugged one shoulder. She didn't exactly relish revealing her vulnerabilities. But again, something told her she was safe in sharing them with Reid.

"I...don't ever remember being told I was beautiful until you said it last night."

"I see." His mouth pulled into a deep frown. "So you've not only dated assholes, but blind ones."

"Kind of. Yes."

"Well, let me be the first to dispel this ridiculous notion." He tucked her hair behind her ear—a sweet gesture she was finding to be uniquely his. "Cute and beautiful are not mutually exclusive. You're honestly one of the most beautiful women I've had the pleasure of knowing, and I don't only mean because you have breasts that make me want to weep with joy."

"Boob guy," she accused.

"Guilty." His serious expression didn't waver. "But you're also damn cute. And if you believed that 'cute' was an insult when I said it before, I apologize and ask that you don't hold that against me now." He pulled her into the circle of his arms. "Your boobs, however, I encourage you to hold against me as often as possible."

She couldn't resist kissing him for that, and when he kissed her back and she melted into him, she knew she was going to break her promise of going out.

They were definitely ordering room service to-night.

Twelve

"How about this one?" Christina held up a frilly-necked shirt.

"Hmm. Not doing it for me." Drew continued sliding the hangers on the rack in search of…she didn't know what.

She'd returned home to Seattle from California on Sunday and now was shopping for her next soft opening. It was happening next week for a sushi restaurant named Soo-She.

She wanted to be prepared with the right outfit for the swanky and minimalist restaurant. The food ranged from traditional raw fish sashimi to inventive new options made with grilled chicken, pork and even steak. There was a lot of buzz surrounding the restaurant because of its unique style—including several VIP floating islands and an open kitchen format that encouraged interaction with the chefs.

Drew was searching for a shirt that complemented the restaurant: noticeable and minimalist. One that made her stand out in case the staff needed to flag her down, but also professional. A shimmery silver blouse caught her eye on the wall, and she was pulled toward it as if by a tractor beam.

"That's the one," she said. "I can pair it with my knee-length slim black skirt and my Choos."

"It suits you. Sparkly and fun." Christina plucked the hanger from its station and flipped over the price tag. "Also, fussily expensive."

"It doesn't matter how expensive it is. I'm buying it." Drew draped the shirt over her arm. "Along with jewelry. I'm thinking a row of silver bangles."

"I'm so jealous of your style. I wish I had somewhere fancy to go." Christina pushed out her bottom lip. Drew had always thought of Chris as pretty, from the moment they'd met last year at the soft opening for the Fig & Truffle on Smithfield. Christina was a waitress at the time, and Drew had been drawn to her take-no-crap attitude. Her friend's style had changed since then. Christina had lost the ponytail, her light brown hair now short and sassy. She favored slacks and striped blouses, and never was without her favorite accessory: a red belt.

"You *do* have somewhere fancy to go. You're coming to the opening of Soo-She, right?"

"Alone?"

"I'll be there!"

"You'll be too busy to babysit me. Is anyone else I know going to this friends-and-family soirée that I can sit with?" They stopped at a clearance jewelry section and began rummaging. "What about Reid?"

"What *about* Reid?" Drew held a pair of hoop earrings to her ear and examined them in the mirror before deciding they were too large for her face.

"You spent several sweaty nights in the man's arms and now you're never going to see him again?"

Drew gave her reflection a wan smile. The latter part of the week had been like a magical fairy tale. She'd let Reid talk her into moving her luggage to his hotel room, and they'd gone to bed together every night and woken up side by side every morning. That second night they didn't make it out to Masala, choosing room service dinner instead, but on night three they did. They ate some of the best Indian food in the city and laughed over shared stories about Gage and Reid's college years.

She'd had sex with Reid every single night. And each time it was mind-blowing and all-consuming. Each time she mused how easy it would be to fall for him. Then she shut down that possibility before she did something she regretted.

Falling for Reid Singleton wasn't an option.

"It doesn't serve me to continue seeing him," she told Christina matter-of-factly. "He isn't looking for a girlfriend, and I don't have time for a boyfriend."

A white lie. She had time, but there was no sense in entertaining a Reid-boyfriend fantasy if it wasn't going to come to fruition.

Christina pointed at Drew with a studded leather bracelet. "If neither of you wants a future, then it doesn't sound like there is any risk to you sleeping together. All I'm saying is that if I could get laid on the regular without strings, I'd do it."

An older woman with tight gray curls grunted disapprovingly as she wheeled by with her walker.

"Oh, like she never used up a man and spit him out," Christina whispered to Drew. "Look at those legs. I bet she was a pistol."

Laughter shook Drew's shoulders as she held up a necklace to her throat. "This would be cute with your navy-blue-and-white-striped shirt. Look, the pendant is a little anchor."

"And half off. Sold!" Christina snagged the necklace and then tilted her head, a look of patience or pity—or maybe both—on her face. "At least ask him to the soft opening. What could it hurt? Invite him and your brother and his fiancée. Make it a group thing. I can sit with them and then I won't have to go by myself."

"Why don't you ask Jerry from work?"

"No." Christina shook her head fervently. "I'm not dating right now. But I'll be happy to grill Reid for you. Is there any intel you'd like to glean? I'll go undercover."

"I'm not sure he'll agree to come!" Drew protested, but she did so through a smile. She did want to see him again.

"Aha! So you *are* asking him."

"Only because we have seats to fill." Drew slipped

a fat, jewel-studded bracelet onto her wrist and forgave herself yet another white lie.

Reid carefully removed the wee cup from the espresso maker, and the surface wobbled dangerously. He sipped the hot liquid from the edge, savoring the coffee he needed more than his next breath. He'd come home from California nearly sexed out and didn't know what to think about that. Not only had he had more sex over the weekend than he'd ever had with one woman in a condensed period of time, but he'd had it with *Drew*.

He'd returned home Sunday night and sent an email to Flynn and Gage letting them know he wouldn't be at the office on Monday. He'd worked from home instead, catching up on email he'd been ignoring. He'd told his friends-slash-coworkers that he was behind because of the mixers and client dinners at the symposium.

The real reason was that he'd spent every spare second over the last weekend-plus in bed with Gage's younger sister.

During the last night they were together Drew had once again sworn Reid to secrecy. She'd brought up the lucid argument that what was done was done and Gage would only worry about her, or worse, lecture her.

"There's a double standard where men are concerned in this sort of arrangement," she'd told him.

He thought it was complete bullshit—to use an American term—and Drew should be able to have

sex with whomever she pleased for whatever reason and without judgment. At the same time, Reid
also saw the situation through Gage's point of view.

Reid wasn't a cad, but he had taken a vow to stay
unwed for the rest of his days. Friends for over a decade, Gage knew Reid better than most. Gage knew
Reid's view on serious relationships—*pass*—and
Reid's dating habits—frequent and fleeting. Now
that Gage had been bitten—nay, *infested*—by the
love bug, he might also believe that Drew deserved
better than a man who would use her for a few nights
of pleasure. Drew meant more to Reid than that, but
he didn't care to have that discussion with Gage,
either.

Now it was Tuesday, and the email was caught up
and Reid couldn't avoid his best friend any longer.

"Morning, Singleton." Gage announced.

Startled, Reid nearly spilled his coffee after all.

"How was vacation?"

"Hardly a vacation." But Reid couldn't deny it'd
been every bit as fun as a vacation. Turned out it was
impossible to be stressed when he spent every evening bare-ass naked, Drew at his side.

"Andy said Drew was there."

"Was she?"

Gage's face twisted into an expression of disbelief. "Yeah."

So probably Reid shouldn't exaggerate.

"Kidding. Yes, she was there. I didn't recognize
her, to be honest. She looked like a different person."

"I talked to her on Monday and she said you

thought her name was Christina and that you tried flirting with her." Gage slapped Reid's shoulder, and Reid nearly choked on his coffee. She'd talked to Gage? And she didn't clue Reid in as to what she said?

"She blew me off," Reid said, careful not to put too much of a gap between the words *blew me* and *off.* She'd paid particular attention to that favorite part of his anatomy Saturday night, and he'd not soon forget it.

"She said you took her to dinner, though, which was nice of you. Thanks for that."

"Not like she's a charity case, mate."

"I'm sure you would've rather been out buying drinks for beautiful women than stuck entertaining my little sister."

Incensed, Reid blurted, "Drew *is* beautiful," even as he reasoned that Gage was her brother and didn't look at her the same way.

"Yes," Gage admitted. "She is. I meant I'm sure you would've rather been servicing the greater part of San Diego than hanging out with Drew."

"You say that like she's uninteresting. I found her lovely." *And receptive, responsive, easy to ravish...*

"You're right, I'm a jerk. I sometimes forget she's a grown woman, you know? I look at her and see a teenager. I overlook the fancy clothes and the new hair color and that air of..." Gage gestured for help. "What word am I looking for?"

"Sophistication."

Gage snapped his fingers. "That's the word.

Who'd have ever thought my sister, who spent her time coloring her hair weird colors and doodling in her journals, would be sophisticated?" He laughed, bemused by his own observation. "Did she call you yet?"

"What? No. Why? I mean, why would she call me?" *Smooth*.

"Yeah, I guess that would be weird. I gave her your number. She invited Andy and me to a soft opening at some sushi joint on Friday night. Asked if you wanted to come, too."

Oh, really? Reid couldn't stop his smile. Seemed Drew hadn't had her fill of him after all.

"She said her friend Christina would be there. *Alone*." Gage waggled his eyebrows meaningfully. Under normal circumstances, Reid's ears would've pricked upon hearing of a woman he didn't know.

Gage watched him expectedly.

Right. Reid should probably feign interest. "What does she look like?"

While Gage described Drew's roommate, Reid swapped his espresso for his cell phone. Thought she'd set him up on a date, did she? Not as long as he had something to say about it. "You'd better give me Drew's phone number. So that I know not to screen her call."

Gage rattled off the number without suspicion. And why should he suspect anything? Reid was a family friend, and news of him running into Drew would be as unremarkable as if he'd run into any other platonic friend anywhere in the country.

Except that Drew had transformed into a goddess who'd wooed the knickers off him.

Except for that part.

Thirteen

Drew sprinkled smoked, flaked sea salt on top of a perfectly grill-marked portion of halibut and assessed her handiwork. She screwed her lips to one side as she examined the green and red sauces. *Too much green*, she decided. She should've left more of the square white plate visible. She balanced a bouquet of microgreens on top of the fish and admired her creation anyway.

There was no Chef Devin Briggs in her kitchen to critique her work, but credit where it was due, he'd given her an eye for plating that would serve her well in her career for years to come.

Fork, knife and napkin in hand, she sat at the kitchen table to enjoy her dinner. Christina was out with her girlfriends tonight, and had been polite enough to invite Drew along, but Drew had passed. She needed a night in to recharge after the social melee of the past weekend.

Her cell phone chimed as she forked the first bite into her mouth. She ignored the text message notification and savored the flavors of her meal. The subtle lemony sauce, the black peppercorns... The chime sounded again, and with a sigh, she dropped her fork.

The first text read: You talked to your brother about us. Followed by: This is Reid btw.

Smiling, she keyed back, Reid who?

Dinner forgotten, she watched the screen for a reply. Two words popped up—Not funny—before the phone rang in her hand. She didn't hesitate for a second.

"Hi," she breathed.

"I'm in the car. Can't text and drive, you know," came Reid's smooth British lilt. Her chest flooded with longing. She'd missed him so much. "You were supposed to call me, Gage said."

"Yes. I was." She ate a bite of fish to stall.

"And invite me on a date with your roommate," he said flatly.

"No, no. Not really." Drew didn't want to think about Reid dating anyone, let alone Christina. The very idea of him kissing another woman made her lose her appetite. "I didn't want him to be suspicious."

"I see. I thought you were sick of me and pawning me off to someone else. I'm not merely a toy to be passed around."

He was joking. She could read him so well now, after just four days together.

"What are you doing after the soft opening?" Reid asked.

"Not much. I typically stick around until the kitchen closes, and then I go home and go to bed. Exciting, I know."

"Are you required to 'stick around until the kitchen closes'?" His voice dipped seductively, and she found herself twirling her hair around one finger as she responded.

"No. My work is done when the guests leave."

"In that case, you can stay the night at my place."

Her heart skipped a beat. Excitement swam through her bloodstream.

"But we were done…after the weekend."

"I've changed my mind."

She bit her lip, a million reasons why she shouldn't be with Reid flickering on the screen inside her head. He was her brother's best friend, and keeping a secret this huge from Gage had already proven challenging. She had no interest in a relationship and neither did Reid, so why continue one? Plus, her brother's wedding next June would be even more awkward if Drew couldn't ignore the crazy, insane chemistry between her and Reid. The smartest tack was to end things now and avoid any sort of romantic entanglement.

But no matter how hard she tried to focus on the future and warn herself of the consequences, the pull to him was too great.

There was only one reason to continue this affair with Reid: because she wanted to.

"Okay," she said. Apparently, that was enough of a reason for her.

"Great. I'll see you on Friday. In the meantime, I have your number and you have mine. So if you're lonesome for me…"

"Reach out?"

"With both hands," he murmured, his accent thick. "Oh, and Drew?"

"Yes?"

"While I'll enjoy unwrapping you no matter what you wear, I really like black lace. Choose your undergarments thoughtfully."

"Yes, sir," she purred.

"Good night, beautiful," he said, and then he was gone.

She ate the rest of her dinner quickly, then grabbed her laptop and glass of wine and curled up on the couch. High-end, sexy lingerie was a click away, and she intended to find the perfect black lace set that would drop Reid's chiseled jaw straight to the floor.

Black lace was itchy.

Or at least the garments she'd purchased were. That's what she got for shopping online for a brand she'd never heard of. Apparently, high price didn't necessarily signify high quality. At the last moment, she'd decided on a slim black dress instead of the shirt she bought for this occasion.

The dress boasted spaghetti straps, perfect since

she loved showing off her shoulders and arms. She worked hard keeping them fit. The skirt stopped just above her knee, and her heels were platforms—sturdy so that she wouldn't slip on the kitchen's slick floors—though she would spend most of her time in the dining room, overseeing tables and communicating to the bartenders, busboys and waitstaff.

She loved the restaurant business. There was an anticipatory hum of excitement in the air as everyone from the dishwasher to the hostess focused on the night going smoothly. They were one cohesive unit, working together for a common goal.

It was exhilarating.

The doors opened to a line out front, and one of the hostesses took the invitations required to enter the restaurant as three other hostesses quickly filled the empty tables. Servers bustled over to take drink orders, and bartenders mixed concoctions in metal shakers with as much flair as they could muster.

"Drew," came a sharp whisper over her shoulder. Christina had shown up early, and Drew seated her at one of the VIP islands that sat four on each side of the chef's station. It was intimate, and in Drew's opinion the best seat in the house. "Are they here yet?"

"I don't think so, but—" Then she saw him. Reid held the door open for Andy and Gage and then stepped in behind them. He was wearing dark slacks that made him seem even taller, a lavender button-down shirt and an eggplant-colored tie. His wavy hair was styled neatly against his head, and you could slice vegetables on that knife-sharp jaw. Her stomach fluttered, and only then did she realize what a bad idea it was to have invited him here. She'd never be able to hide her attraction to him. She was glowing like a neon sign.

"I see Gage!" Christina said excitedly, then, "Oh... my gosh. Drew. *Drew!* Is that him? The guy—the model-looking guy? Is that Reid?"

"That's him." Every wide, tall, capable inch of him was glorious to behold.

Gage pointed in Drew's direction and walked over, and as much as she tried to keep her eyes on Andy's friendly smile, her gaze strayed to Reid. Reid winked at her, his hands in his pockets like he hadn't a care in the world.

She couldn't believe in a few short hours she'd be going home with him. It was heady. It was amazing. It was—

"Hey, sis." Gage pulled her into a hug before turning her over to Andy for another hug. She turned to greet Reid next, but then didn't know what to do. Offering her hand for him to shake seemed formal. He erased the need for her to overthink it as he embraced her gently.

"Drew. Good to see you again," he murmured before placing a kiss on her temple. "You're looking well."

Was it hot in here or was it her? One more look at Reid, and she disagreed with herself. It was him. Most definitely.

"This, uh, this is my roommate, Christina," Drew introduced, and everyone said a quick hello.

"Ah, the *real* Christina. Finally, we meet. Did you know Drew impersonated you to an entire symposium filled with potential clients?" He kissed Christina's hand and she giggled, dissolving like any woman would with Reid's attention squarely on her.

"I begged her to go in my place. I was dying of the plague, but I've made a miraculous recovery."

"I can see that." He held Christina's hand for another beat before letting it go and taking the chair right next to her. Drew frowned, not liking that at all.

"Go do your thing," Gage told her, and then said to the table, "Take a good look at her while you can. When Drew's at these things she's running ninety miles a minute and barely stops to be cordial to the people she knows.

"It's true," Christina agreed. "She has focus like I've never seen. It's like she's powered by the energy surrounding her. I've never seen someone so turned on by food."

Christina didn't mean it in any other way than it sounded, but with Reid smiling at her, all Drew could think about was that once, in her not-so-distant history, she'd been turned on by food exclusively, and in an unhealthy way. What didn't help was that her roommate had never had such a problem.

Christina was narrow and tall, her limbs delicate and graceful. She *barely* worked out and had been blessed with a metabolism that would make any woman jealous. She was also taller than Drew by about four inches, and even in a plain ensemble of slacks, a striped shirt and a red belt, the other woman seemed to *fit* with Reid better than Drew.

At times like these Drew felt as if she were playing dress-up. Like she was faking her success in her new clothes and new hair and new body, and soon the spell would be broken. The clock would strike midnight and she'd transform into the shy, unconfident girl with a bigger waistline. The second that thought walked to the front of her mind, her hard-won confidence flagged.

"I love sushi," Christina told Reid, her smile beaming. "Don't you?"

"I love to eat just about anything," he said with a healthy dose of his typical charm. Christina giggled.

Drew ignored the blaze of jealousy in her chest. She trusted Christina, and being charmed by Reid was inevitable. He was a potent mix of masculine attributes. The man could woo a nun out of her habit.

Drew excused herself and left her friends and her brother to their evening. She had a job to do. Before she disappeared into the kitchen, she stole one final glance over her shoulder.

Reid's eyes were glued to Christina.

Fourteen

Christina, on Reid's left, leaned to make eye contact with Andy on Reid's right. "Tell me more about your wedding next year. Drew said it was going to be in Ohio?"

"Crown, Ohio. At a vineyard. With a lake." Andy's smile brightened her entire face. She chattered about the venue excitedly, how it'd be a weekend-long affair and how each of her sisters had been married at the same lake. "It's a family tradition. It's also where Gage and I fell in love. You probably already heard about that."

"Drew mentioned that you two pretended to be together, even though you barely knew each other." Christina's eyes snapped to Gage.

"The connection was instant," Gage said with a

man-in-love's smile on his face. "There was no denying it."

Reid swallowed thickly as he recalled the first time he'd seen the "new" Drew on that dance floor. Recalled the way she'd moved in that skirt, and those shoes he couldn't tear his eyes from. The way she'd approached with a bubbly confidence that had drawn him to her.

Like a moth to a flame, Janet Jackson sang in his head.

Even if Reid could've written off the encounter as sheer physical attraction, that excuse fell flat after he'd figured out who Drew really was. Hell, moments before he'd recognized the birthmark he was musing over the connection he'd had with the beautiful brunette.

"...and your plus-one, of course," Andy told Christina, sending a lingering, meaningful glance at Reid. "Whoever that might be."

He'd zoned out and missed a hell of a conversation. He blinked over at Christina, who looked visibly uncomfortable. "Oh, well. You know. I don't... um...thank you for the invite."

"We liked the idea of having a joint bachelorette/bachelor party at the lake," Andy explained. "Reid'll be there."

Ah, hell. They were trying to set Reid up with Christina. Yes, he'd been flirting a little to reroute the attention from the way he was reacting to Drew. Apparently, it'd worked a little too well.

But a wedding *one year* in the future? *Andy, dar-*

ling. Evidently Gage wasn't the only one infested by the love bug. In the interest of not making things awkward, Reid played along with her Cupid-like intentions.

"I wouldn't miss your commingling cock-and-hen party. I enjoy a good F-you to tradition." Reid raised his glass of sake and said a cheers to everyone at the table.

The chef at the center of their cozy table served their sushi rolls and bento boxes. Gage struck up a conversation about the skill it took to create their food, and Andy leaned on her elbow and smiled, listening as the chef talked at length about his training. Reid used that opportunity to turn his back to friends.

"Sorry about that," he whispered to Christina. "It seems they believe we belong together."

"Yeah, well, if you weren't laying it on so thick, we might not be in this mess. You'd better not talk to every girl like you're talking to me. Drew is a good person."

Reid couldn't help smiling. He liked that Christina was standing up for Drew. "You're a good friend. I didn't mean to oversell it."

"You can't help it, I guess." Christina picked up her chopsticks and lifted a crab roll. Around a mouthful she added, "Look at you."

"Can't a man be polite without being thought of as a player?"

Vehemently, she shook her head, gesturing to him with her chopsticks as she chewed. "You're great-looking. Not good-looking. *Great.* I imagine attention from the opposite sex isn't hard for you to obtain."

"You make it sound criminal." Her comment peeved him, probably because it'd sounded more like an accusation. He grumpily ate a piece of sushi.

"It's not criminal." Christina returned to her meal. "But it certainly doesn't make me feel special. Is... *you-know-who* special?"

"Of course she's special." Reid had known Drew for years—true, he hadn't seen her in several of those years, but she was related to one of his closest friends. She automatically meant more to him than a stranger. Was Christina implying he'd taken advantage of Drew? Simply used her up and spat her out?

"She's a good person," Christina reminded him again—as if he needed reminding.

"I know that." The muscles in his neck went taut. He'd graduated from peeved to pissed off.

"She deserves more than a playboy is all I'm saying."

The thread of his patience snapped. "Why don't we enjoy our dinners and attempt to survive tonight as amenably as possible?"

"Reid." That scolding whisper came from the woman at his right elbow. He turned to meet eyes with Andy, whose auburn eyebrows climbed her forehead.

"He's fine, Andy." Christina smiled. "It's my fault for bringing up football."

"Reid hates American football," Gage paused eating his own dinner to say.

"I—I know. That was the disagreement." Christina leaned out of view of Andy and Gage to mouth "sorry" to Reid.

Reid leaned over his food to shield them from Andy's and Gage's prying eyes. "We need to be more convincing than this. For Drew's sake."

He'd already vowed not to speak to Gage about what'd happened in California and, given Christina's presence, it wasn't hard to guess that Drew wanted to keep up the ruse.

He guessed there was a certain logic to keeping mum. This thing between him and Drew would be short-lived. She didn't want a boyfriend any more than he wanted to be one, or so she'd confessed that last morning they'd spent together. It'd been an unwelcome goodbye. When she'd offered a kiss on his cheek and whispered, "Don't worry, Reid, I won't make this weird," he'd felt an odd pang of regret that their time together was well and truly over.

Only now it wasn't. As long as no one was the wiser that Drew and Reid were together, all would end well.

Christina threw her head back and laughed, making it a point to touch his arm. "Oh, stop!" She laughed again heartily and sent him a meaningful nod.

Right. They needed to be more convincing.

"Well, you asked," he played along, pasting on a wide smile. At that same moment, he saw Drew pause in the mouth of the kitchen, a stricken expression on her face.

Bloody hell.

"Um, pardon me for a moment." He stood from his seat and angled for Drew, who tore off through the dining room. He caught her in the hallway leading to the restrooms.

Snagging her upper arm, he tugged her deeper into the corridor. Thankfully, they were on the opposite side of the restaurant from their friends, and out of sight.

"What are you doing?" Drew shook out of his grip.

"Coming to explain that I am not flirting with your roommate. Well, I am," he amended, "but not because I want to."

Drew folded her arms over her breasts—God, those breasts. He had to mentally will his attention back to the conversation he'd started. At least they were alone for the moment.

"You don't seem too broken up about having to flirt with her," Drew said. "Apparently, you've got her eating from your hand."

"She threatened me two seconds ago," he said in her roommate's defense—and a bit in his own. "If you want to blame anyone for this situation, blame yourself. You're the one who doesn't want to tell Gage the truth."

"You didn't seem to have a problem agreeing with me. What's the matter, Reid? Worried that my brother will lose his hero worship for you now that you've stooped to have sex with someone like me?"

What the—?

If Reid was upset before it paled to the rage roaring through his bloodstream now. How dare Drew talk about herself that way? And what the hell did she mean "someone like her"?

"Stoop?" He wheeled her backward and they bumped into a door that read Employees Only. He tried the knob, hoping someone had been careless. As luck would have it, the door opened. He shoved them both inside the pitch-black closet and shut the door. He flipped on the light switch, illuminating the cramped space in a yellow glow. Stacks of paper towels, takeaway containers and other items towered on shelves lining the small closet.

"I do not stoop, Drew." He pressed her back against a blank wall. "*Ever*. Are we clear?"

Some of the anger bled from her expression, leaving behind beautiful, raw vulnerability. Whatever issues she had about her worth were her own. He'd do well remembering that. But he wasn't above teaching her a lesson.

"Unless by stoop you mean…" He dropped to his knees and pushed her skirt up her thighs.

"Reid! What are you doing? I'm at work."

"Proving you wrong," he answered as he slipped her panties off. "Or right, depending on your perspective."

He hiked the dress up over her hips and buried his face between her legs. She sagged against the wall, her fingers twining in his hair. Soon, her incoherent noises mingled with low moans of pleasure.

She tasted like heaven when she came—the same

way she'd tasted last weekend. He'd missed being with her already. That wasn't normal for him.

He ignored the stray thought and placed another loving kiss on her most precious part before standing to his full height.

She blinked heavy eyes at him as he tugged her dress down, then she frowned as if belatedly realizing an important component of her wardrobe was missing.

"Panties." She held out a hand.

Pretending to be angry with me? I know better, love.

He thumbed the scrap of black lace and then shoved the garment into his pocket. "I believe I'll keep these as a souvenir of our time together tonight. Whenever you catch me play-flirting with Christina I want you to remember my lips on, well, *your* lips, quite frankly."

Her mouth dropped open into a stunned smile. She liked him slightly crass and under her command. That much he knew.

"And then I want you to remember that I have your underpants in my pocket. That I came to find you, kiss you and drop to my knees at your feet." He pressed a firm kiss to her mouth. "That, *love*, is the only time I stoop."

On that brilliant parting line he left the closet, brushed the dust off the knees of his trousers and walked out to rejoin his pretend date for the evening. He stuffed his hands into his pocket and touched the lace panties he wished he'd gotten a better look at in the dim light of the supply closet.

No matter. That was only a preview of what was to come this evening. Specifically, *Drew*. As many times as she'd allow him to take her to the edge and over.

Fifteen

Reid was spent.

Through and through, just an absolute goner.

He'd told Gage and Andy he'd take a car home, wished Christina well, and then he'd waited at the bar with a scotch while Drew finished up. She had, in what had seemed like record time, and was gliding over to him in the black dress that rocketed a punch of anticipation straight to his gut. He'd put his arm around her and kissed her temple the moment she was close enough for him to do so, and then he'd put his lips to her ear and whispered, "Missing something?"

Knowing he was referring to her panties, she'd laughed and her cheeks had turned pink, and that'd simply made his night.

Or so he'd thought. What had *actually* made his

night was bringing her to his apartment, sweeping aside her dress and shoes, and taking her to orgasm half a dozen times.

"Doesn't seem fair that you can have six of them while I only get the one," he teased. He was still lying flat on his back in bed. She was out of sight, somewhere in his walk-in closet, where she'd disappeared a few minutes ago.

"Six what?" she called from the recesses.

"Orgasms."

She stepped from his closet wearing one of his navy blue button-down shirts. The tails came to her thighs, and she was fiddling with one of his striped ties, attempting to knot it at her neck.

"I think it's fair." She paused in her task to grin, all pearly whites and mischief.

He sat up and scooted to the edge of the bed, gesturing for her to come to him. When she was standing between his legs, he finished knotting the tie for her.

"Have an important business meeting to attend?" he joked as he tightened the tie at the collar of the shirt. He liked her this close, her breath dusting his cheek. There was something about Drew that towed him in. Her inherent sweetness, perhaps…

Or her lack of experience.

If he thought too much about that, he'd feel a heap of guilt, so he shoved it aside.

"I like your clothes." She stepped away and held out her arms to show off her outfit. Navy blue shirt, tie and the shiny black heels she'd worn tonight.

"I like you in my clothes." He'd been allowed

to spend another evening pleasuring this amazing woman. He was a lucky bastard.

She stepped toward him in the exaggerated walk of a model on a runway, before losing her nerve and laughing.

"If you had any idea how sexy you looked doing that, you wouldn't laugh."

She shoved the shirtsleeves, which had swallowed her hands, to her elbows.

"You're good for my ego." She patted his cheek, and he caught her hand, the words *You're good for me* on the tip of his tongue.

He didn't say them, figuring she'd take them the only way she knew how—to mean more than they actually did.

Though he wouldn't be lying. Drew *was* good for him. It was he who wasn't good for her. She was sweet and open, learning about all life had to offer her, and from what he'd seen tonight, life would continue delivering more to her capable hands.

In the restaurant, she'd been poised and confident, impossible for him not to admire. Even while pretending with Christina, he hadn't been able to keep from stealing glances at Drew. But he'd seen the girl she used to be beneath that womanly exterior. That bashful, sweet girl who had much more potential than she gave herself credit for.

Reid, on the other hand, was jaded, broken. Not a good prospect for a commitment. As long as she wasn't with him long-term, she had a chance at having a full and complete relationship with someone else. He'd not rob her of the chance to be more, have more and do more.

Arguably he was taking advantage of her weakness for him to fill a void that had been cavernous since he was a child. It was unfair, but he also believed in Drew's strength. She'd recover from him in no time at all. He'd see to it.

"Do you miss London?" she asked out of the blue. "Your family? I'd miss my family if they weren't a car's ride away."

"Sometimes," he answered honestly. Family wasn't a topic he liked to discuss with anyone—not even his closest comrades, Gage, Flynn and Sabrina. And he most certainly hadn't traipsed down Family Lane with any woman in his life. Oddly enough, Drew felt like a safe zone for Reid. Again he thought about how they'd "connected," and as perplexing as it was for him to admit he felt that way about her, he couldn't deny it.

"That was the heaviest 'sometimes' I ever heard." She stroked his hair. This time of year was always hard for him. His birthday was around the corner, and there was no way to avoid what came with it. The past. The memories. The sorrow.

"You know, in spite of your rakish reputation, Gage never warned me about you. And I'll bet he never threatened you to stay away from me, either."

Reid blinked away the thoughts of his family's tragedy to focus on Drew. There, in his shirt and tie, looking for all the world like a woman who belonged in his bedroom. Typically, a woman in his bedroom was doing one of two things: asking for more or putting on her clothes to leave. And that was because *typically* he wouldn't have lingered in the bedroom. He'd have kissed her lightly and made the excuse that he couldn't sleep. Then he'd hide behind his laptop at the dining room table until she fell asleep or decided to call it a night.

He hadn't thought too hard about that before now. He'd seen it as polite; a good way to avoid awkward conversations about family, friends, past or future. But with Drew, he'd lingered. Hell, he hadn't even gotten dressed.

"You're correct," he told her. "Gage never warned me off."

"Know why?" She loosened the tie. "I was never on your radar. And he never told me to stay away from you because he knew I didn't stand a chance of winning you. You've always been out of my league."

He caught the length of silk around her neck and pulled her to him, then threw the tie aside and unbuttoned the top two buttons of the shirt she wore.

"To be fair, I never had the chance to see you outside of a family gathering." He kissed the space between her collarbones. "One normally doesn't prowl family events in search of a date, you know."

"*Ew*. I'm not family."

"You were eighteen, Drew. You'd just graduated from high school, were ensconced with friends your age and had no interest in me whatsoever."

She clucked her tongue, which told him he was dead wrong about that.

"And I was an idiot twentysomething who wouldn't have dreamed of hitting on you lest Gage have my ass. I couldn't have acted on my attraction if I'd stopped for a second to allow it to form." He cocked an eyebrow. "How was I to know you'd morph into a foxy siren who knows exactly how to turn me on?"

"Or that I'd avoid any gathering where you'd possibly be present?"

"No." He frowned, not liking the sound of that.

"Gage and I don't have a lot of friends in common, so it didn't come up often. But, yeah, I was sure to tell him to arrive at soft openings with a date and not a friend, just in case."

"Just in case what?"

"Just in case." She shrugged one shoulder and didn't give him any more than that.

"Just in case," he repeated as he unbuttoned another two buttons and parted the shirt. "I saw you and couldn't contain myself?" Her breasts, large and full, sat on display before him. He sucked one nipple and then the other as she raked her nails into his hair. After a minute of leisurely exploration he wasn't sure who was enjoying it more.

"Seriously. You are *so* good at that." She moaned, the earlier topic forgotten. Which he preferred. He didn't want to hear her reason for why she hadn't wanted to bump into him. Given her comment earlier about him "stooping" he could guess it wasn't a positive one.

He rested his face between her breasts and, his

voice muffled, proclaimed, "Anytime." When he lifted his eyes to hers, she was smiling down at him.

Much better.

She pulled the shirt closed and crawled into bed. Content to stay a while longer with her, he moved to settle in at her side.

"Regardless of what we do or don't do together, you know you can talk to me, right?" she asked.

"About?" He half expected red emergency lights to flash or a siren's wail to pierce his eardrums at the inference of "talking." Definitely, he should climb from bed and beg off to work. *Talking* was never a good idea, but he didn't budge.

"Anything."

"I have nothing to talk about." He tucked her dark hair behind her ear, loving the silken feel of the strands. "I prefer you as a brunette."

"And in black lace," she added.

"Yes. But mostly *out of* black lace." He wrapped his arms around her and kissed her, and she shoved against his chest gently.

"I'm a great secret keeper. I never gossip. I don't share privileged information."

"Christina knows about us. Not so great, I fear."

"We weren't together when I told her. You were part of my past. Completely fair game. How can I be sure you won't spill the coffee beans to your bros? To *my bro*, in particular? You and Gage are like this." She crossed her index and middle fingers to illustrate. "He'll pry it out of you eventually."

"I'm a better secret keeper than you, guaranteed."

She harrumphed.

"I've kept a secret from Flynn, Sabrina and Gage since I met them. I've never once 'spilled the *coffee beans*.'" He grinned at the cute way she switched up the phrase. He'd learned over the course of spending several mornings with her that Drew liked coffee almost as much as he liked her breasts.

And that was saying something.

"I don't believe you." She jutted her chin stubbornly.

"Drew. I once swore an oath on my tallywacker that I wouldn't wed and never broke that pact even though *both* Flynn and Gage pussed out. Believe me. My word is oak."

"I'm already trusting you to take the you-and-me secret to your grave."

Unbeknownst to her, that phrase was apt when it came to the other secret he harbored. A shadow stretched over the room and consumed him with dark thoughts.

"You can tell me what happened, Reid." She played with the wavy hair atop his head. "Be brave and tell me about the girl back home who broke your heart."

He met her seeking gaze. A decade was too long to harbor a secret from friends. He'd sworn years ago that he'd tell them eventually, but the timing was always wrong. When was the best time to bring up tragedy? He still didn't know when he'd tell Gage, Flynn or Sabrina, but his gut told him now was the exact right time to talk about Wesley with Drew.

"You're completely wrong," Reid told her, his eyes losing focus as his gaze slid away. "It wasn't a girl back home who broke my heart. It was my twin brother."

Sixteen

"Twin brother?" Drew had no idea he had a twin brother. "Are you two estranged?"

"He died. We came to believe."

Her heart sank to her toes. She didn't understand what he'd meant by that, but he seemed ready to talk about it, so she was here for him. She rested a hand on his chest in silent support.

"He disappeared during our birthday party." Reid shoved a pillow under his neck. His gaze was on the ceiling, but she didn't move into his frame of vision. She sensed this wasn't a story he told often. He'd probably appreciate her presence more than her sympathy.

She waited for him to continue, idly stroking her fingers through his chest hair and watching her own hand rather than staring at him. Eventually, he must've felt comfortable, because he spoke again and didn't stop for a long while.

"It was a hot afternoon. I don't know how, at three years old, I remember that. But I do. Mum and Dad planned a massive circus-themed birthday party. It was packed with face-painting clowns, jugglers, a petting zoo. Mum had insisted on a huge inflatable castle packed with plastic balls. When I could get her to talk about the day, she'd tell me how she'd fought for that inflatable with Dad for a week solid before he'd given in. He'd thought it a monstrosity."

Reid smiled at the memory, and even though it was sad at the edges, it transformed his handsome face. He looked at once older and younger.

"Within a half hour of the festivities and among legions of neighborhood friends, my twin brother, Wesley, went missing." Reid sucked in a breath, but it barely lifted her hand where it rested on his chest. As if the oxygen hadn't quite reached his lungs. "Dad dived into the in-ground pool to look for him there, just in case Wes had fallen in. I don't remember that part. But he told me that he'd had a vision of Wes at the bottom of that cement box, blue in the face. When he came up out of the water to an expectant crowd of onlookers, he shook his head and they dispersed.

"The search party blanketed the yard, the surrounding neighborhood and the patch of woods beyond the house. It wasn't a large area to canvass, but everyone came up empty-handed. Police took over the search at nightfall, blanketing an even bigger swath of land. They'd interviewed the clowns and the jugglers, the animal handlers. None of them had any idea where Wes was. No one saw him wander off."

Reid paused to swallow, his Adam's apple bobbing as if pushing past a lump of dread. Drew's stomach turned in anticipation of the story that wouldn't end well.

"Five years later—"

"Oh my God," she couldn't keep from whispering.

"—my folks decided to have a funeral. Trying to find Wesley had become their life. They'd gone on television to share the story, had been interviewed by papers and had covered the surrounding towns and villages in posters with Wesley's photo on them. My mother was a functioning alcoholic by then, having turned to the bottle when the grief became too much. My father was simply exhausted. He'd told me he'd never felt so impotent in his life not being able to protect his family.

"I can relate to that. I couldn't protect Wes, either. I was too small, just as helpless, but I'm older and when I grew up I still felt... I don't know. *Responsible*. It's hard being the one left behind and feeling as if a part of yourself died, as well. I know everyone believes that my reasoning for the pact not to marry has everything to do with sowing my wild oats forever, but it's more about what I've to offer someone. To be honest—" he slid his eyes to her, his face a mask of sadness "—I don't have a lot left to offer."

"Oh, Reid." She hugged him close, holding him

until his breathing returned to normal instead of shallow bursts. "I'm so sorry."

"Thank you. By the way, Mum's graduated from drinking daily to drinking occasionally."

"So she's well now?"

"Yes." He frowned like he didn't want to say more, but then he did. "Sometimes I wonder if life would've been better if my dad had found Wesley at the bottom of that pool. I'd give anything to have my brother back, but if it had to happen then—if I could choose the way he'd die—it'd be that. We have no idea what happened to him. His body never turned up. He was simply…gone."

Her heart snapped clean in two at the anguish in Reid's voice.

"And you've dealt with it by keeping quiet."

"Not too bright, eh?" He smiled over at her, but it was forced. She touched his chin, resting her index finger in the dent there.

"I won't tell Gage. I won't tell anyone. No matter what. I swear."

"I trust you." He squeezed her against him and kissed her forehead. She loved being this close to him, being held by him. It made her feel safe. She liked being the person he could rest his burdens on, too. "Though it's probably time I told my friends about my brother. They think I don't like aging and that's why I never allow them to make a fuss over my birthday. Truth is, my family doesn't celebrate it. We haven't since the day we lost Wesley. After the funeral, it felt like a betrayal to continue celebrating. Every day I'm on this planet is a day he's not."

Oh, Reid. That guilt must've eaten a hole through his gut like battery acid.

"You've never told anyone this," she said.

"No. What I just told you was more than I've admitted to family, to friends."

"Girlfriends?"

"I don't have girlfriends. For reasons you've now gleaned."

"I always wondered why you weren't a one-gal kind of guy. Now I know." She could understand how he'd become gun-shy. His parents sounded like part of them had died alongside Wesley that ill-fated day. Reid must've felt overlooked, soaked in all those negative vibes as a child, all while struggling to understand what had happened to his brother.

"I still feel him." Reid's mouth tugged down at the corners. "That's the strange part. Like there's a chip embedded here—" he pointed to the center of his chest "—and I can still sense Wes somehow." A quick jump of his eyebrows dismissed the subject. "You must think me barmy."

"Barmy?" That was a new one.

"Crazy."

"Ah. No. It's not crazy. When my grandmother Adele died, I was fifteen years old. I had dream after dream about her. In those dreams, she always said the same thing. 'Look for me in the sky, Drew. I have my wings.'" She smiled at the thought. "Every time

I see a bird, a butterfly or a bumblebee, I say to myself, 'Hello, Gran.'"

"Sweet *and* cute."

He shook his head. "Definitely you deserve better than me."

"Why don't we not talk about who deserves what when it comes to us?" She wanted to sooth and comfort him. Wanted to see his easy smile return even though she knew there was a shadow hiding behind it.

"What shall we discuss, then?" His smile wasn't quite easy but it was there. Evidently he was ready to cast off the bleak topic. She knew just how to do that.

"I should amend that we aren't talking about who deserves what unless we're talking about orgasms, which I can hereby state with clarity that I need a minimum of six each and every time you and I are naked together. Even though it's unfair for you and your pitiable one at a time." She poked her bottom lip out into an exaggerated pout, and Reid laughed. It was a small laugh, with barely any breath behind it, but she considered it a win.

"It's not my fault I'm much better at delivering than you are, love."

"Not funny!" She swatted him with the sleeve of the shirt she wore, belatedly realizing it was going to be unwearable if she continued wrinkling it. She sat up abruptly. "I should hang this up."

"Wrong. You're not leaving this bed." He was on top of her in a flash, pinning her down and tearing open the shirt. She let her eyes wander over her own nude body, at her large breasts with nipples pointing at Reid as if saying, "Here we are!" Her legs and thighs, while not perfectly slender, had plenty of muscle. She admired the way her smooth skin was juxtaposed against Reid's hard planes, thick thigh muscles and wiry hair on his legs. She marveled at the heavy penis brushing against her tender sex.

"Make love to me." She flexed her arms uselessly since he held her wrists. "I need it. And so do you."

His eyes held weighted darkness behind them. She couldn't erase it any more than she could fill the empty part of him, but she could help take his mind off his loss.

And maybe that's what they were to each other, a way to forget the past and heal parts of themselves that no one else could. Her by being the person he needed most right now, him by being the only man who could fulfill a decadelong fantasy for her.

"My pleasure." He kissed her, accepting her offers—spoken and unspoken—and taking them to the pinnacle of passion yet again.

Seventeen

Drew sipped her coffee and tried her damnedest to wake up. When she wasn't participating in an opening for a restaurant, she worked from home scheduling, interviewing and planning the next opening. Even on a Sunday like today, she'd normally be awake and handling her email. She hadn't so much as made it to the shower yet, and it was almost ten o'clock.

Reid had kept her up way too late doing amazing things to her body she wouldn't soon forget. She shivered, her tired smile resting on the edge of her coffee mug.

Friday night after the opening at Soo-She, he'd told her about Wesley. Last night she'd cooked for him at her place—chicken piccata—and he'd stayed the night. Christina had gone away for the weekend, leaving the house blessedly empty.

Drew had managed to get out of bed an hour ago, but hadn't wanted to wake him with running water and the sound of the blow-dryer.

She'd lingered in the doorway of her bedroom and admired the sculpted, firm globes of his solid buttocks, the muscles in his back and how good his dark wavy hair looked against the bright white of her bedsheets.

Reid Singleton in her bed, bare-ass naked, wasn't a sight to rush. So she'd stood there until she felt like a creeper and finally forced herself into the kitchen for coffee.

She'd been there since, but after cup number two failed to motivate her she wondered if she should give up and crawl into bed next to him.

"Morning," came a raspy male voice from the hallway. Reid was in the gray T-shirt and worn soft jeans he'd arrived wearing, but he hadn't bothered with socks and shoes. And his hair was finger-combed by the looks of it.

"No fair. No one should look as good as you do in the morning."

"Hah. Nice try. Where's mine?" He gestured to her coffee, and she pointed at the mug on the counter. "Thoughtful," he praised as he poured himself a cup. He took the chair next to her at the kitchen table. She had one leg curled under the other, her heel resting on the edge of the seat. He wrapped one big, warm hand around her toes.

"What's on your docket today?" Much as she'd love to lounge around in her apartment with Mr. Perfect Ass, she really should get to work.

"Sundays I head to the market to find something to eat for the week. I drop off my dry cleaning. The usual exciting weekend stuff. You?"

"Work."

"On a Sunday?"

"Yeah. I work from home a lot. It's a gig that can't only be handled nine to five, Monday through Friday."

"I suppose that's true. I've always been grateful for my nights and weekends free. It's the appeal of Monarch and being your own boss."

"I thought Flynn was your boss."

"Well. We let him believe he is." Reid grinned.

He was too damned charming for his own good. And far more layered than she ever would've guessed. She'd only ever seen a fun-loving, hotter than Hades Brit who was utterly unattainable. Now that she'd been with him on multiple occasions, she saw how unfair she'd been to him. He was human, with feelings and hurts and a past that was darker than any of them knew. She'd never sensed anything ominous surrounding him, but she supposed she was too busy keeping her distance to have noticed.

"When is Christina returning?"

"Tonight."

"My place, then? You can bring your work if you need to. No sense in both of us running off in the morning." He sipped his coffee while he checked a weather app on his phone. "Eighty-four degrees today," he mumbled almost to himself. As if he felt the weight of her stare, he met her gaze. "What?"

"For a guy who doesn't want to be involved with a woman, you make a lot of plans with me."

"Am I to believe you're finished with me?" He raised one cocky British eyebrow. "I'm to believe you want nothing to do with me and your pending six orgasms tonight?"

"Are you so content to let me use you?" she teased with a giggle, but there was some truth to what she was asking. She didn't feel the least bit used by him. He'd made her feel like a princess, and had soothed her most tender spots since the night he'd found out her true identity.

"Yes." He narrowed his eyelids. "Perhaps we should outline a few ground rules to keep from getting in too deep."

"It's not a bad idea." She wasn't accustomed to open-ended anything. Her next six months were planned to the minute. Her dated planner was decorated in washi tape and appointment stickers. Her to-do list was bullet-pointed and detailed. "How about we set an end date?"

"Okay." He nodded as if this was par for course, an idea that made her slightly uncomfortable. Nevertheless, she pressed on.

"Probably before the holidays." She couldn't imagine sneaking around during Thanksgiving or Christmas. The guilt of lying to her brother and family would eat her alive. "Should we count Halloween as a holiday?"

"Are you invited to any costume parties?"

"I go to at least one every year."

"And we don't want to navigate couple *costumery*."

"I'll be busy that entire month anyway. I'm opening three different restaurants."

"Very well. That gives us August and September."

"When...um. When's your birthday?" She felt uncomfortable asking since she'd learned it was a sore topic, but she couldn't not ask. Reid didn't have a single good birthday memory and she wanted him to have one. One he could be happy with and not overwhelmed by.

"September fifth."

"I can't believe you told me that."

"Neither can I." His eyebrows jumped in a show of adorable self-deprecation before he stood from his chair. He finished his coffee and bent to place a kiss on her forehead. "I have to run. Tonight? My place?" At the sink he rinsed his mug. He looked in her kitchen.

My place in your life?

"Tonight. Your place," she confirmed.

"Uber will be here in a bit," Reid said of the car service coming to pick him up. He gathered his things from the bedroom, and she met him at the front door.

"Seeing me out?" he asked. "So sweet."

"And cute. I know. I know." She rolled her eyes, but she didn't take offense to him thinking of her as "cute." Not now that she knew "cute" and "sexy" weren't mutually exclusive.

"Damn cute," he agreed in a low, sexy murmur. Then he kissed her, holding on long enough to make her want to grab him by the shirt and drag him back to bed. He hummed softly as he ended their kiss and pulled open the door.

There, in the threshold, stood Gage, fist raised to knock.

"Reid?" Gage's eyebrows crashed over his nose, then he snapped his attention to Drew. "What the hell?"

"What are you doing here?" She tried to keep her voice steady, but it wobbled slightly.

Her brother lifted a foam cooler. "Dad came into town and left this. You know I eat fish as rarely as possible. I only did that Soo-She thing because they offer a chicken option."

Their father worked at a fish hatchery in Leavenworth, Washington. He often brought his work home with him and more often brought his work to Drew and Gage.

"Why is Reid here?" Gage asked, again skewering his best friend with a glare.

"Because, dummy," she stalled. She always went with confidence when she had no idea how to escape the predicament before her. "He was visiting Christina." She waved a hand at Reid, who gave her an incredulous look. "I don't understand his appeal, but whatever."

She crossed her arms over her chest and shrugged. If confidence didn't sell it, indifference would.

"I thought you and Christina didn't work out." Contrary to her accusation, Gage was no dummy. It was up to Reid to back her up. Drew almost doubted he would. It was one thing to keep a secret from her brother, but it was another to lie to his face. She sent telepathic messages to Reid asking him to support her white lie with one of his own.

"Well, it may not last, but it worked out for the night," Reid said, charm oozing from his every pore. "Don't wake her. She had a long, *long* night," he told Drew, going as far as to point toward Christina's empty bedroom.

"I won't." Even though they were pretending, she felt a spike of jealousy at the thought of Reid and Christina having a long night together. Which made no sense, so she flashed Reid a quick smile of thanks and then took the cooler from Gage. "Thanks for the fish."

"Where you headed?" Gage nodded at Reid.

"Home. My car will be here—" he consulted his cell phone's app "—in two minutes."

"Cancel it. I'll give you a ride home."

"You're sure?"

"Positive."

Reid pressed a button, declared that it was "done" and resumed his walk out the door. "Let's go, then. Drew, always a pleasure."

She bit her lip, hoping with all she had that Gage wouldn't grill Reid on the way home and that she wouldn't have to hear a lecture from her big bad brother about how Reid wasn't the man for her. Gage might think he knew his best friend, but after last night she knew him better.

She shut the door behind her brother and her temporary boyfriend and sagged against it for a full minute. She'd been taken advantage of by men in the past, and there was no doubt in her mind that Gage would see this as another mistake in the making. He would worry she'd fall in love with Reid the way she had with Devin, and before him, Ronnie, and before him…she didn't even want to think about how many romantic mistakes she'd made in the past. And since Gage knew his friend was as unobtainable as plucking a star from the sky and putting it in her pocket, he'd have warnings for her—and probably a few for Reid about what they were doing together.

The trouble wasn't that Gage would be wrong to worry, the trouble was that he would be *right*. But she had a sixth sense about Reid. Even though she'd just agreed to an end date and even though Reid had professed himself unable to have a long-term relationship, she believed he could come to mean more to her than either of them had ever dreamed.

He'd already been a better boyfriend than Devin and Ronnie combined. And he hadn't even been trying.

Her eyes sank closed. She couldn't—wouldn't—allow herself to fall in love with Reid Singleton. No matter how amazing he was in bed or how sweet he could be in the morning. No matter that he'd shared his broken, sad past, trusting her with that information and no one else. She could keep this light and walk away unscathed. That would be best for both of them.

"Keep telling yourself that, Drew," she said on a sigh. Then she walked the kitchen to put her freshly delivered fish in the fridge.

Eighteen

"Thanks for the lift," Reid said, breaking the stifling silence. If it weren't for Drew's insistence that they keep the affair from her brother, he'd just as soon tell Gage what was going on. Reid was a grown man; he could handle whatever his best friend had to say. And Gage could use a reminder that his sister was a grown woman, whether he wanted to admit it or not.

"Christina is an odd choice for you." Gage kept his eyes on the road, his mouth firmly set.

"Is she?" Reid tried to sound bored, but some of his irritation bled through.

"Yeah. You usually gravitate toward bubbly and bouncy, and Christina is neither of those things."

"Opposites attract. I suppose your and Drew's matchmaking worked."

"Uh-huh." More silence infiltrated the car.

"What is it, Gage? Stop being so damned stubborn and say what you're thinking."

"Drew is…she's an adult and I know that. But she's also a lot like she was when we were growing up. There's a new, hard-won confidence to her, but there is also a naive side. She believes in dreams coming true and fairy tales, and it's gotten her into trouble in the past. With men."

Reid hated thinking of Drew with any of the *gits* she'd dated in the past, but he couldn't exactly show his anger lest he tip his hand.

"She seems to be holding her own fine now. How do you know she's not seeing someone?" Reid grumbled. "Does she tell you everything?"

"She tells everyone everything about the guys she dates. Although after the way Mom gave her hell about the chef who dumped her, she might be keeping quiet. You were at her place, did you notice her texting someone a lot? Any phone calls? She's been acting differently these past two weeks. She seems… happier."

"And you're unhappy about that?" Reid asked his friend, trying not to gloat over Drew's happiness. He liked knowing he'd brightened her world. She'd shined a spotlight on his, as well.

"I'm not unhappy she's happy, I'm wondering how long this one will last before it fizzles out and I have to go over there with Ben & Jerry's dairy-free ice cream, or gelato and help her through another devastating breakup. I can't bear to see her hurt again."

Gage let out a sigh, and Reid felt his friend's concern for Drew in that gust of air. Gage loved his sister more than anyone. Reid knew what it was like to love a sibling that much. He could relate to feeling their pain like his own. Why should it be any different between Gage and Drew?

"Worrying comes from my mother's side, I guess. I should stop being such a pussy, yeah?" Gage tagged Reid's arm. "Anyway. You and Christina make a good couple. She's smart, and she's adorable. She's been fiercely loyal to Drew, which I appreciate. Did you know she moved in with Drew last year after the Devin Briggs debacle?"

"No, she, ah, didn't mention that." Reid frowned in thought. He didn't know much about Drew, actually. He didn't usually know a lot about the women he dated. Knowing a lot about them opened up the conversation to them knowing a lot about *him*, and he tried to avoid that sort of depth if possible.

Until Drew. She knew an awful lot about him. More than he'd meant for her to know. His time spent with her had dredged up his painful past and was making him face his biggest fears, but he could swear…it was ridiculous but it seemed as if…she was *healing* him.

"You okay? You look, to use your term, completely *knackered.*" Gage grinned, proud of his Britishism for "tired."

"I am knackered," Reid admitted.

"Christina wild in the sack, is she?"

"Keeps me on my toes," Reid answered with a

wily grin. This was territory he was comfortable with when it came to nattering away with his friends. Sex was fair game, and he often had tales of prowess to tell. Gage would expect no less.

"She's a firecracker. Multiple orgasms, right in a row." He snapped his fingers. "Bam, bam, bam."

"Nice." Gage nodded his approval, but Reid doubted he'd be nodding his approval if he knew they were talking about Drew.

Drew had been right in the assessment of her brother. Gage loved her, but was overly protective of her. He believed she was bouncing about falling in love with any git who came to call, but Reid knew differently. He and Drew had made an agreement to end this affair—they'd even given it a time line.

Drew wasn't going to be sobbing into her ice cream when Reid walked away. He wouldn't allow it. Besides, she'd already seen some of the bones in his closet and he doubted she wanted to see the rest of the skeleton.

He'd take the gift of spending time with her and in turn make it the best of her life. And hopefully teach her a thing or two about how she should be treated by the next man who enters her life. He'd make sure she knew that no one less than Prince Charming was worthy of her, and he'd make sure she understood as much when they kissed goodbye for the final time.

It was all in a day's work, he lied to himself. *No less than what you'd do for any other woman in your bed*, he argued.

What bothered him all the way down to his bollocks was that whenever he thought of saying good-bye to Drew, a bit of loss snuggled in next to the bit that resided in his chest. Drew, the perfect yin and to the yang of Wesley. He'd miss her. But he would let her go when it was time.

"Anyway, sorry for pumping you for intel," Gage said. "I just want Drew to find someone who treats her with respect."

And treats her to multiple orgasms, Reid thought with a smile.

Drew carefully folded the final French crepe and stacked it on top of the others.

"I'm ridiculously excited to eat." Reid rubbed his hands together, all but drooling at the sight of the tower of fluffy, thin crepes.

"I love feeding people. Because of that ravenous look right there."

He snagged her waist and pulled her onto his lap. She nearly upended it onto her own lap before resting it safely on the table. "Careful!"

"Never," he proclaimed before sliding her hair aside and kissing her neck. He wrapped his hands around her front and cradled her breasts, fingering her nipples through her thin T-shirt. After they'd had sex on the sofa, he'd complained he was "famished," and she offered to cook for him. When she went to get dressed he argued that he didn't want her to put clothes on. She'd explained the dangers of cooking naked, and he'd allowed the clothes, but only if "you sleep next to me without them."

It wasn't a hard-fought argument. She'd agreed immediately.

"Now what?" he asked as she slid from his lap to sit in the chair at the table next to him.

"Now you fill them with berries." She demonstrated by lifting a delicate crepe onto her plate, filling it with a line of macerated strawberries and blueberries and rolling it up like a skinny burrito. "And then…" She reached for a can of spray whipped cream and wrinkled her nose. "This is sacrilege but since you have no cream to whip, we'll have to make do." She squirted a dollop of whipped cream onto her crepe and then held the can between them. "Do I want to know why you have this in your refrigerator?"

"Probably not."

"Ugh."

She reached for her fork, but Reid caught her hand. "I'm *joking*. I have it because I like it on my ice cream sundaes."

"Oh."

"Sounds like your filthy mind had a better idea."

She felt her cheeks warm, and she smiled at her plate. "Maybe."

"I promise to save some for later." He cocked an eyebrow and then filled his crepe, topping it with whipped cream and digging in. She stopped eating to watch him eat. Watching the way he closed his eyes, moaned in appreciation and sagged in his chair like he'd been overcome. "Why are you planning restaurant openings when you should clearly be head chef at one?" He forked another bite into his mouth and caught her staring. "Something wrong?"

"No. Not at all. It's just…I've never told anyone this but lately I've been writing recipes, designing menus. Instead of fussing over schedules like an underpaid party planner, I'd much rather be wooing people's taste buds with my creations."

"Well, you should," he said simply, and then pulled another crepe onto his plate to assemble. "These are incredible."

She watched his long, blunt fingers as they rolled the crepe. He had such a sure and strong way about him. Talk about confidence. She couldn't imagine there was ever a time he didn't have it. But that time had existed, hadn't it? Only in leaving London and finding friends in Seattle had he escaped the oppressive atmosphere of living with parents who mourned his twin brother.

"Why don't you do it?" he asked.

"Do what?"

"Open a restaurant."

She chuckled. "Most restaurants fail, Reid."

"Fig & Truffle restaurants seem to do okay."

"They're a huge corporate conglomerate. They have a safety net wider than the Pacific Coast."

"So open a restaurant with them. Like Soo-She or whatever. You can call it, I don't know, Drew's Diner."

"I don't want a diner. I want a fancy eatery where every morsel is more mouthwatering than any you've tasted before."

He held her gaze for a protracted moment before finally saying, "Sounds like you."

She blushed again. She'd never get over this gorgeous, godlike man flattering her.

"You know during the ride home, Gage mentioned that he thought you were seeing someone. He was worried it'd be another wanker like Devin Briggs. Or the guy before him."

"Ronnie."

"Whoever." Reid dismissed the topic with a wave of his fork before digging into his second crepe. "Your brother worries about you settling. You shouldn't do that."

Reid regarded her sincerely. Kind of like when he confessed about Wesley, there was no cover-up, no cocksure tilt to his mouth.

"I *don't* do that."

"Do you want a family, Drew?"

"What kind of question is that?" She busied herself taking another bite while she decided how to answer. "Not now. Right now I want a career I love. I want a relationship with someone who understands I have to work to make my dreams happen. I want—" She cut herself off when she knew the end of that sentence. *I want to be with someone who encourages me to pursue those dreams.* Reid had just plainly told her that she should be creating menus and cooking for a living and that she should go for it.

"Of course not right now, but eventually, I can see you with a family man. The trick is to find a man who fits that bill at the right time. Someone who loves and respects you and wants to put down roots."

She chewed a strawberry thoughtfully before asking, "Do you want a family?"

"Never." There wasn't a second's hesitation in his answer.

"How can you say never?"

"Easy. I watched mine turn to dust. It's not a pretty sight. The only family I need is the one I have in Gage and Flynn and Sabrina." He opened his mouth and shut it again, like he decided not to say more. She wondered if he was going to include her in that "family" label but had changed his mind. Because they were sleeping together? Or because soon they wouldn't be, and friends was too big an ask after all they'd done together?

"You're worthy of your dreams, Drew. Don't let anyone talk you out of them, whether it's a chef who wants to pigeonhole you, or a guy who's obviously not cut out to be who you'll need him to be in the future." Reid rested his hand on hers, his expression one bordering on regret. Like maybe the second guy he mentioned was himself.

"Thanks, Reid." She squeezed his hand and smiled.

"You're welcome."

They went back to eating their late-night snack, and she thought about how Reid was wrong about who he was, if that's who he'd been referring to. He was capable of being who she needed in the future.

He was who she needed right now.

Nineteen

Using the key entrusted to her from Fig & Truffle, Drew unlocked the Market location of the elegant restaurant. It was a standalone building just off the pier, facing the water with an amazing view of the sunset.

Inside, the restaurant was polished to perfection, deep red-brown woods and pale cream-in-coffee painted walls. The floors were charcoal gray, the chairs a tasteful blend of neutral colors. The soft opening for this location of Fig & Truffle was soon, so Drew considered herself lucky that her boss agreed to let her borrow it.

She held the door open for Christina, who followed with a cup of strong coffee they'd picked up on their walk to the pier. It was the ungodly hour of 7:00 a.m., hours before the management team came in here to train the myriad servers, cooks and other staff who would have this place humming like a well-oiled machine on opening day.

"It's beautiful." Christina ran her hand along one of the smooth vinyl booths. "This is my surprise? I thought it was this." She held up her coffee cup.

"Well, the coffee was a bribe to coax you out here with me." Drew walked to a darkened corner of the restaurant and flipped on the lights. Soft orange-yellow bulbs spotlighted the tables. "I'm borrowing it." Christina had slid into one of the empty booths across from the bar, her eyes on the neat rows of liquor bottles lining the wall. Until Drew added, "For Reid's birthday."

"Excuse me?" Chris pegged her with a stern glare.

"I talked to my boss, and his boss and a few other bosses, and then I begged a little and they agreed to lend me the restaurant, a chef, a server and a bartender for Reid's birthday dinner. I'm thinking gold and black streamers here." Drew pointed to the bar. Then she gestured to the table where Christina sat. "Candlelight, black place mats and gold chargers, and Fig & Truffle's signature square white plates and bowls. Reid and I will have the entire place to ourselves."

"Drew, honey." Christina's face was a mask of concern.

Drew could guess what was coming. She'd already shared with her roommate that Reid didn't celebrate birthdays, which, to Drew, was a crime. Sure, he had a good reason for not celebrating, which she *hadn't* shared with her friend, but she couldn't bear the idea of another birthday passing him by without creating a new, happier memory.

"It's just the two of us," Drew reiterated in her own defense. "I'm not going to invite a hundred people or anything."

"Yes, but is this your place? I mean, even though you two are…" Chris waved a hand. "Whatever you are to each other."

"We're together…for now. That's what matters."

The month of August had flown by in a blur of happiness. She and Reid saw each other every night during the weekends and two to three nights during the week—whenever she didn't have to work in the evening. She'd mostly stayed at his place, toting her laptop with her. She'd spent her mornings off lounging on his fantastic L-shaped sofa and drinking espresso from the machine on his counter that was even more expensive than the one she'd splurged on for herself.

She cared about him. Deeply. And knowing that his birthday was a source of pain for him, she wanted to do something for him no one else had done. His family might not believe it was important to celebrate the day of his birth, but Drew did.

She knew from their many conversations that Reid wasn't ever in a relationship for long, yet he'd been with her almost two months. They'd agreed to end things this month, but she couldn't let him go without showing him how much better things could be.

He'd suffered cut-to-the-bone pain when he'd lost his twin brother, but the future didn't have to be so bleak.

She wanted to help him. And while she knew throwing him an intimate birthday dinner wouldn't heal him completely, she thought it would be a good start.

"Isn't he going to be upset with you for doing this?" Christina's brow dented with concern.

"He doesn't know what it's like to be celebrated, Chris. Everyone deserves that. He spends so much of his time telling me I'm worthy and capable. It's past time someone did that for him."

Her friend smiled. "You're a great person, Drew."

"So are you. Because you're going to help me decide on a menu." Drew hustled to the hostess station and grabbed a leather-bound menu. Back at the booth where Christina sat sipping her coffee, Drew slid into the other side and pushed the menu across the table. "Steak, fish, or should I go out of the box and choose something like lamb or pasta? Chicken seems too pedestrian."

Reid's birthday was two days away and she was very aware that this little dinner celebration was close to their farewell. Neither of them had talked about it lately. She wondered if he'd changed his mind about "getting in deep" with her. She already knew she was in over her head.

"Why are you asking me instead of a chef?" The pained look in Christina's eyes suggested she already knew.

Drew sighed in defeat. "Because the chef can't advise me how to tell Reid I'm in love with him. And I was hoping you could."

Christina reached over the menu to grasp Drew's hand. "I thought you were breaking up soon."

"This month, though we didn't set a specific date."

"I guess... I don't know why you're doing this."

"Reid deserves an amazing birthday celebration. I can't say why, but I can tell you it hasn't been a happy occasion for him for most of his life. If I can give him the gift of a happy memory when he turns thirty-two, I know he'll appreciate it more than he'll ever be able to say."

"It's sweet, Drew. It's amazing." Christina shook her head sadly. "That's why I'm friends with you. Because you're sweet and amazing and you do these incredible acts of kindness for those you love."

"I'm sensing a 'but.'"

"But." Christina smiled softly. "If you're not sure that Reid loves you, too, you're taking a really big risk. You know things are ending soon, and since he's a man it's not hard to guess that he's taking whatever you're telling him at face value. He thinks you're all in for the good time you're having. *Without* strings."

"I am." Drew tugged her hand away. "I absolutely am. But that's the point. I'm in love with him and I suspect that under the playboy facade—that's not even the right word for him—he cares for me a lot. Why would we call this quits if it's working so well?"

"This plan isn't only about his birthday, is it?"

Drew pressed her lips together, debating how to answer that question. If she said no it would be as honest as she'd been with herself while she was planning the entire thing.

"It's *mostly* about his birthday," Drew said. "It's also about showing him what could be possible if we leaned in *a smidge* more." She measured out half an inch between her index finger and thumb and held it in front of her face, watching Christina though the gap.

Drew couldn't help how she felt, and she couldn't deny she wanted more. She wanted more nights in Reid's bed. She wanted more snuggling on the couch. She wanted more Sunday mornings making him scrambled eggs and cups of espresso. She wanted to tell everyone that he was hers.

Including her parents, Gage and anyone residing on planet Earth. She was hopelessly in love with him and wanted everyone to know it.

"I'm tired of keeping us a secret. We're worthy of good things, and finding each other was the ultimate good thing."

"I know. It really has been," Christina surprised her by saying. "I'm all for banging the Drew-and-Reid-forever drum. What I don't want is for you to go in with expectations that aren't what Reid wants at all. I don't want to see you hurt when you're on the totally opposite shore from him. When he does exactly what he says he would do, and you blindside him."

"What's that supposed to mean?" Adrenaline poured through Drew's veins, taking her buoyant mood with it. She sensed her friend was about to share an unwelcome observation. When Christina said, "Hear me out," Drew knew she was right.

"Didn't Devin tell you several times while you dated that he wanted to travel and have a family? Hadn't he been exploring being a personal chef and working with a few wealthy families overseas the entire time you two dated?"

Drew frowned. "Yes, but—"

"You told me he was done being in Seattle. You told me all he talked about was not being stuck in a restaurant kitchen."

"If you're taking his side—"

"I'm not taking his side, Drew. I'm taking *yours*. He told you exactly what he wanted and you told me that you didn't want that. You wanted to be here in Seattle. You wanted to build your Fig & Truffle dream. You wanted to be career-minded and rock the foodie scene. Devin left you and it was a rotten thing to do. Just terrible, but he did exactly what he told you he wanted to do."

"We could've compromised."

"You were clear with him about what you wanted. He tried to change your mind. Did it work?"

"You're not helping!" Drew sprang out of her seat and paced the length of the bar. "I'm over Devin. I'm with Reid. This is about Reid!"

"It's about you, too, sweetie. You want him to go along with how great the two of you can be together, but he's already stated exactly what he wants. You can't dazzle him into changing his mind with the ultimate Pinterest birthday celebration. Tell him you love him *before* you try this tack."

"No. I have to *show* him. I have to show him that this is what we can be." Drew rested her hands on the table. "Chris, I told Reid I wanted a restaurant of my own and he told me to go for it. I made him crepes and he saw my potential. But I had to show him. He sees me in a way no one else does. He just doesn't know what he's capable of yet. I'm going to bring him here on his birthday and show him what our future could look like. Trust me."

Christina nodded, but she looked unconvinced. So much for backup. But no matter what her friend thought, Drew was as certain of her plan as she was of its outcome. Once she wooed Reid with a perfect evening, once she gave him the gift of a second chance at a real, meaningful relationship, she knew he'd see things her way. They had potential—a truckload of it—and she wasn't going to let him go when it was so obvious they belonged together.

"Steak or fish?" Drew nudged the menu.

God bless Christina, who perused the options before meeting Drew's seeking gaze. With a sigh, she said, "Tell me more about the ribeye with thyme butter."

Twenty

Lost in thought on the code he was writing for work, Reid didn't hear Gage come in. Reid jumped when a black box with a white ribbon landed on his desk in front of his keyboard. He surfaced from his concentration and allowed the two computer screens in front of him to recede into the background—after first hitting the save key. If he lost even a line of coding, he'd tear his hair out.

Gage stood at the other side of Reid's desk, arms folded over his chest. "That's for you."

"What for?" Reid took off his glasses and set them aside.

"Your birthday, dimwit."

Reid stared up at his best friend, half in shock, half in irritation. Gage knew as well as anyone that

Reid didn't like celebrating his birthday. Gage and Flynn used to give him shit about it, but they'd eventually stopped.

"Since I'm not allowed to give you birthday gifts, consider this my official bribe."

"Bribe?" Reid popped the ribbon and opened the black box, revealing a watch inside crafted completely of wood. He'd never seen anything like it. "This is incredible. Why does it smell of whiskey?"

"It's made from bourbon barrels."

Points for being unique, Reid thought, impressed.

"What's the bribe for?" He took the watch from the box, admiring the style. The numbers 12, 3, 6 and 9 were burned into the wooden face. The weight was nice, the size perfect, and the metal clasp a brown-tinted stainless steel. He snapped it around his wrist.

"It's also water-resistant in case you jump into the lake at the wedding with it on. The bribe is that I'm making you my best man. I know you don't do the wedding thing. Hell, I don't do the wedding thing. But Andy and I are doing the wedding thing, Reid, and I need you at my side."

Reid never wore his emotions on his sleeve. He preferred acting aloof to vulnerable, ever the sincere smart-ass. In this case, however, he couldn't hide his happiness for his friend. Before he thought about his actions, he was out of his chair and wrapping Gage in a manly hug, and slapping his back for good measure.

"I'll do it," he vowed, and then because old habits died hard, added on, "but only in case you change your mind about being married and need a ride to the airport."

Gage clapped Reid's arm and laughed, taking the comment the way it was intended. "Yeah, yeah. Anyway. I'm giving Flynn a flask. He's my other best man."

"You can't have two best men." Reid feigned offense. Flynn and Gage were like his honorary brothers, and he didn't mind sharing the spotlight with Flynn a bit. "I'm clearly *the best* man because you came to me first."

"Luke's going to be in the wedding party, too. I'm running out of friends," Gage said of Sabrina's brother. "Andy has five sisters and they're all in it, and my side's a little light. How weird would it be to ask Sabrina and Drew to stand up on my side?"

"Drew?" Reid croaked. "Drew. Right. Of course. She's your sister, after all. You should absolutely include her."

Gage frowned. As well he should. Reid had gotten emotional, which he never did, and then overreacted about Drew, which he never would've done had it not been for the sneaking around with her on the regular.

"We'll figure it out. Maybe do something nontraditional like have everyone walk down the aisle in pairs. Like, you and Drew could walk together, Flynn and Sabrina, and then Luke can escort one of Andy's sisters... I don't know. We haven't figured it out yet."

Reid nodded, his mouth as dry as if he'd just eaten sand. Walk down the aisle with Drew? It shouldn't be awkward, but since he'd been sleeping with her for the better part of the past two months and knew the end was nigh, it might be weird to see her next June. What if she had a date? What if *he* did?

Gage was blissfully in the dark, having given up the notion that it was odd finding Reid in Drew's apartment. He'd asked about Christina a time or two when they'd been out for beers. Reid had played it off, saying they were doing "okay" and then adding that he wasn't "ready to let this one go yet" in case Gage popped in at either Drew's or Reid's house and caught them together. At least if the Christina lie was in circulation, he'd have a prayer of playing it off.

What was making him so damned uncomfortable with the situation wasn't keeping Gage in the dark, though that was inconvenient, but that Reid had started suspecting Drew was on the brink of wanting more. He'd had enough experience with women to know when it was time to pull up. Drew might not be in love with him yet, but she was close.

Every time they were together, there was a lot more than sex between them. They'd become friends—close friends—in a short time, and had shared secrets and stories with each other. Making love with her was healing a deep wound that'd occurred when Wesley vanished, and no other woman could claim the same.

Reid swiped his brow, sweat popping out on his forehead. He had to get out of here, just for a while.

"I, um, I forgot." He put his computer in sleep mode before grabbing his bag and stuffing his laptop into it. "I have to be across town for a thing."

"What thing?"

"Meeting with a guy—it's too boring to talk about. Probably why I forgot." Reid cleared his throat and checked the time. It was nearly two o'clock. "Yep, running late. Thank you for the watch. It's already come in handy. June. I'm excited."

With that off-kilter farewell, Reid and Gage stepped out of the office. As Reid locked up, Yasmine, their assistant, called Gage over. Reid used the distraction to bolt to the elevator, but not before Sabrina stopped him on the way.

"Hey. You okay?" She was wearing her black-framed glasses today and a royal blue dress that made her green eyes appear even brighter.

"Perfect. Late for a meeting."

"Oh, well, I'll let you go." She pointed at his wrist and smiled. "I see Gage asked you to help marry him." She winked, and Reid felt something loosen in his chest. No sense in being dramatic about it. What was with him today? He wasn't big on premonitions, but he felt as if someone'd walked over his grave.

"Yeah. He did ask." He gave her a smile.

"And you said yes." She beamed. "I'm glad."

"Me, too."

"You set a date yet?"

"Not yet, but we will." Her smile brightened. "Are you eagerly anticipating standing up at our wedding, too?"

"You know me. I never miss a good wedding."

"Uh-huh." She chuckled and turned for her office, calling over her shoulder, "Have a good one, Singleton."

He smiled to himself, shaking his head at his own bout of random anxiety—which he considered perfectly normal now that he thought about it. His birthday was tomorrow, after all. It'd been an off day for his family for as long as he could remember.

Drew had invited him to dinner on his birthday. Fig & Truffle at the Market was opening soon, and the staff was doing a practice run even before the soft opening. They needed extra mouths to feed, and she'd invited him since she knew he wouldn't be busy. He'd warned her not to sneak in a birthday celebration, and she'd sworn by drawing an X over her left breast that she'd do nothing of the sort. He trusted that to be true. *It'd better be true.*

Surely, she knew after he'd shared with her the tragic loss of Wesley that a surprise party wasn't a good idea.

Besides, he had further reasoned, she'd have to invite Gage, Sabrina and Flynn, which would mean telling them about the relationship. He doubted any of his marriage-bound friends would be happy to hear about them—especially when they found out Reid and Drew were temporary.

Tired from the afternoon slump, Reid drove to Brewdog's, deciding that a hot drink and some time alone with his laptop was in order. He needed to escape the office and have a bit of solitude. Solitude in public. Coffee, or maybe a cuppa, sounded incredible right about now.

He stepped inside, displeased to find a line. Figures. This week had been a kick in the bollocks all the way around.

Almost all the way around. Drew had been the highlight of his night on most nights. He hadn't seen her in a few days, which shouldn't have been a big deal but here he was, standing at Brewdog's wearing a watch made of bourbon barrel, feeling melancholy and displaced, and missing her. Missing her because she knew how to take his mind off his troubles. And it was about more than her shedding her clothes— though that certainly took his mind off *everything*. Drew knew when to needle him, when to push, when to sit back and wait for him to speak. She also cooked a mean omelet. He'd found risotto unimaginative and dull until the other night, when she fed him a bite she'd cooked on the range in his kitchen. Truffles truly changed everything.

She was becoming special to him in a way that he hadn't been able to fathom. How about that?

Lost in thought, he wasn't aware the line had moved until the guy behind him tapped his arm and murmured a polite, "Excuse me. The line's moving."

Reid shuffled forward and turned to apologize but stopped cold when he found himself looking into blue eyes that were eerily similar to his own. Actually, *everything* went cold. His face, his hands, his arms. The laptop bag he was holding felt as heavy as if he'd toted in a cinder block. The sounds around him receded, replaced by a high-pitched hum inside his head.

The man who'd tapped him cocked his head

slightly but before he could get a word out, Reid felt tears prick the corners of his eyes.

"Wesley?" His voice was barely audible over the chatter of the café, a dry croak of sound he'd desperately tried to make audible. Every part of his being, every cell within, told him that the man with eyes that matched his own was his deceased brother.

"Tate." The man shook his head and offered what might've been an uncomfortable smile. "Tate Duncan."

He offered a hand, and Reid stared at it for a beat longer than appropriate before taking it in his own. "Reid Singleton."

On contact, "Tate's" face went slack. They stood there, hands clasped, staring silently for an awkward beat before Reid let go.

"Next customer," the barista called out. "Sir?"

"Um, right." Reid faced the barista, determined to shake the eerie moment. "Americano. Two pumps vanilla." He gestured to Tate and said, "Put his on mine."

"You don't have to—" Tate started.

"I insist."

Tate let out a small laugh and then gave his order. "Black coffee."

It's a coincidence, Reid told himself as he paid. The shake in his arm receded, his limbs warming as the cold sensation went away. It didn't change the certainty in his gut, though.

Reid and Wesley weren't identical twins, but they'd had the same eyes. Their mother had dressed them in matching clothes at that age, and even now they didn't look that dissimilar, each in chinos and button-down shirts.

Reid watched Tate from his periphery as he walked to the other counter to await their beverages, and that gut certainty that this man was Wesley back from the dead returned with a sickening twist. And Reid had no idea how to broach that topic without sounding like a complete and utter loon.

"Thanks for the coffee, man." Tate's accent was American with a dose of cool, calm California. Not a note of English in it that Reid could detect.

"You're welcome." Reid swallowed thickly, trying to reason a way to keep Tate from leaving. To tell him that he was not Tate, but the twin brother who went missing on their third birthday.

Reid *knew* it.

"Do we…know each other?" Tate laughed awkwardly. "I usually remember everyone, and I can't get over the familiarity. But your name doesn't ring a single bell. Sorry if that's rude."

"No. You're right. We do know each other." Reid spotted the hairline scar beneath Tate's right eye and once again, reality tilted on its axis. Wesley had been bitten by the neighbor's nasty poodle a few weeks before their birthday. The scar had been an ugly one and had required stitches. It was now faint and white and exactly the spot Reid remembered from the many photos their parents kept around the house.

He couldn't let Tate leave this café without telling him the truth.

"You're not Tate," Reid blurted, knowing he sounded bonkers.

"An Americano and a coffee, black," called out one of the baristas.

Tate grabbed the drinks and handed over Reid's cup, offering yet another polite smile. "I am. Trust me."

"Trust *me*. You're not." Reid cuffed his brother's arm and moved him aside, feeling the resistance in his younger-than-him-by-two-minutes twin. He spoke quickly, afraid to pause for even a second and lose his nerve. "You're Wesley Singleton and you were born in London. Your birthday is tomorrow. Your mother's name is Jane and your father's name is George and I'm Reid—" he cleared his throat "—your twin brother."

Despite the stark shock on Tate's face, and the onlookers who paused to take in the dramatic scene, Reid pressed on. He had one shot to get through to his brother or he would never see him again. He knew it in his bones.

"Our third birthday party was a circus theme and there were clowns," Reid continued. "And jugglers an-and a big inflatable house filled with plastic balls. And a pool!" He knew how he must look: wild-eyed and crazed. He didn't care. He'd spent his entire childhood looking at children his age for any sign that they were Wesley. There'd been a feeling so strongly within him at the funeral that Wes hadn't died. That he was alive and well. Over the years he'd lost hope, but he wouldn't lose Wesley again.

"Listen, please. There was a pool, Wes." Reid tightened his grip on his brother's arm. "And your favorite toy was a Curious George soft toy and I threw it into the pool once and Mum dived in with all her clothes on to get it for you."

"Look, man…" Tate's expression turned thunderous as he shook out of Reid's grasp.

But Reid was nowhere near giving up.

"You went missing," he told Tate as calmly as he could manage. "We looked and looked. For years. Your funeral was five years after that, and we buried an empty casket. I have no idea how you're here and why you don't sound like you should, but you are and you don't. I know as I stand here that you're not Tate Duncan. You're my brother, Wesley Singleton."

Tate's face had gone stark white; his blue eyes were wide and frightened.

"I don't mean to scare you." With one shaking hand Reid pulled a business card out of his bag and thrust it into Tate's palm. "Try and remember and then call me if—"

"Look, buddy." Tate's voice shook with anger. "I appreciate the coffee but whatever scam you're running, I'm not interested."

"Wait, Wes—"

"It's *Tate*. Leave me alone." He looked at the business card gripped between his fingers and then tossed it, along with his untouched coffee, into the nearest trash can. "Don't follow me or I'm calling the police."

Twenty-One

Tate Duncan's hands were shaking so badly on the steering wheel of his Mercedes he considered pulling over at the nearest curb and waiting for the sensation to pass. Instead he kept his hands wrapped around the leather and took in what he could see, hear, touch and smell.

His name was Tate Duncan. His parents were William and Marion Duncan. His fiancée was Claire Waterson.

He'd been adopted—and yes, he'd had an accent when he was a toddler. But his birth mother had given him up for adoption after his father had died, and then she'd died shortly after that. He had his birth parents' death certificates, for Christ's sake.

"Scott and Natalie Winters." He spoke his birth

parents' name aloud in the car, his voice sounding hollow and desperate. If what the stranger in the café had said to him was true, then that meant… what…his adoptive parents had lied to him his entire life? Or worse—had they arranged to have him kidnapped?

"It's ridiculous," he said aloud, but his body betrayed him and the shakes in his arm started anew.

He pulled into a hotel parking lot. He was in town on business today to finish up the plans for his new build on Spright Island, but now he'd rather take the ferry home and have the damn plans sent by courier.

Fear and confusion swam in his bloodstream. The run-in with Reid left behind enough doubt that Tate touched the screen on the dashboard of his Mercedes and called his parents in Santa Clarita.

"Hi, sweetheart," his mother's voice said over the speaker.

"Mom."

"What's wrong? You sound like something's wrong." Always the sensitive sort, Marion Duncan detected a problem immediately.

"I'm going to tell you a story, and I don't want you to interrupt until the end." He carefully recounted what had happened at the coffee shop, sharing every detail except for one. What he didn't tell his mother was that when that Reid guy shook his hand, Tate felt such a sense of peace it overwhelmed him. It was like seeing an old friend after years apart. And that, he realized, was exactly why he'd called his mom to tell her about what had happened. "Then I threw away the coffee and business card and walked out."

Tate raked his hands into his hair and waited for the silence to be interrupted by his mother's chiming laughter. He hoped with every fiber of his being that she'd tell him Reid sounded like he was in need of psychiatric attention. Then she'd reassure Tate that everything was fine and tell him not to worry, and they'd talk about something else.

Like his birthday plans for tomorrow night.

Your birthday is tomorrow.

How the hell had Reid known that? It had to be a scam. That was the only reasonable explanation.

"Mom." He said her name insistently, praying that the call had dropped or there was some other reason for her silence.

"Tate, honey," she managed, her tone so grave it sent chills skittering down his spine. "We need to talk."

Twenty-Two

Drew was so excited she could burst clean open and out would spray gold confetti. Her smile had been incurable most of the day as she picked up the final details for Reid's birthday dinner.

She'd decided to call the chef she'd hired for the night and ask his specialty. Turned out it was a gorgonzola New York strip steak atop pureed vegetables and garlic potato wedges. It sounded so incredible she ordered the same dish for herself.

Once the meal was decided, the only plans left to complete were decorations. Black and gold was the theme, and she'd spent the past hour hanging foil streamers and tying balloons to the barstools. The table was set in black and gold and white, and she planned on soft jazz as the background music.

Once the restaurant was set and the staff of three had arrived, she changed in the women's restroom. She'd chosen a red dress for the evening, forgoing her habit of being modest by wearing a plunging neckline. That, as much as the rest of tonight, was part of her gift for Reid.

She was excited about giving him a new memory of his birthday. One that would stand out in his mind and make him smile. He'd know that she cared about him enough to make the effort, and, she hoped, he'd also have a glimpse of what their future together would look like.

The past, however, was a tricky beast. Even in her current state of well-being and confidence, she had moments of fear and anxiety, and deep-seated feelings of not being good enough or pretty enough or worthy enough.

Reid was a reminder that anything was possible. That the dream she'd once harbored in the quiet of her heart had come to fruition. They'd found each other at the perfect time, and she planned on showing him that tonight.

And then she was going to tell him she was in love with him.

She checked her phone, but no word from Reid despite her earlier texts. She called in case he was driving. No answer. She settled on sending another text: Starting at 7 sharp. Does that work for you?

She watched the screen for a few moments but then decided not to be weird about it, filling the time by turning the lights down low and locking the front door. That way, Reid would have to let her know he was here, plus she didn't want a person off the street disturbing her private party.

At five after seven she checked her phone again. Nothing.

She called. No answer.

He could've been held up in traffic. Maybe his phone died. Reid had never played games with her before, and had always done what he'd said. She knew he hadn't forgotten.

Unless…

She chewed her lip, remembering her early-morning text to him. She'd wished him a "happy birthday" followed by a "can't wait for tonight!" At the last second, she'd added a heart emoji to her text and sent it.

Surely that wouldn't have scared him off?

"He's on his way," she said aloud. She refused to let her confidence do a free fall. Tonight was too important to give into timidity.

At nine o'clock, Drew gave up the hope she'd held so dear. He wasn't coming.

She locked the door behind her borrowed staff, Beaux, Dana and Rocko, apologizing again for the hiccup in plans. Fear and worry mingling in a volatile mix, she lifted her cell phone and tried one last time to call Reid. After the fourth ring her heart sank, and this time she left a voice mail.

"Reid. It's nine o'clock. I'm at Fig & Truffle. You didn't call, you didn't text. You didn't show up. I don't know what to think. I'm scared to death you've been in an accident. I'm probably overreacting. Things happen. Delays occur. Hell, maybe you had a family emergency. Anyway, happy birthday."

She pressed End and stared at the screen of her phone, her stomach churning. She was worried, but she was also pissed. Was this his way of ending things? Was he going to ghost her until she went away? It seemed cruel, especially after how certain she'd been that they were growing to love each other, but…

Maybe Christina had been right.

Drew hadn't come clean about her feelings to Reid, and now he didn't show up to the evening she'd planned.

"Or…" she told herself. "He's reeling because it's his birthday."

Reid had not only shared the truth about his deceased brother, he'd told her plainly that birthdays weren't celebrated since Wesley's disappearance and subsequent funeral. Reid had warned her off from planning anything, and she'd told him not to worry, assuming he'd be grateful once he'd arrived. She'd convinced herself that she was doing this for him, *for them*, but was she? Or did she become so wrapped up in the planning that she never stopped to think about what he wanted?

Christina was absolutely right. Drew hadn't leveled with him about *anything*.

Reid must've caught wind of her plans, or maybe he'd sensed via her texts and the heart emoji that tonight wasn't a soft opening after all. If he'd suspected her of luring him here for a birthday celebration— one he hadn't asked for and didn't want—there's no way he'd show up.

She'd accept her share of the blame, but he should've communicated his feelings—no matter what they were. He could've at least given her the courtesy of a reply text.

"Bastard," she growled under her breath. Anger took the controls from worry as Drew drove to Reid's apartment. She vowed to keep a cool head and let him say his piece, but if she found out he'd blown her off on purpose, they were going to have a lot to talk about.

Short of death, there was *zero* excuse for him not contacting her to tell her he wouldn't be there tonight.

She banged on Reid's door after sweet-talking the front desk—Ralph knew her by now, so it hadn't been that hard—but there wasn't an answer. She knocked one last time before trying the knob, and the door opened.

Inside his apartment she heard the TV around the corner, and took a deep breath of relief when she saw him sitting on the couch. Now that she knew he was okay, she was going to kill him.

"It's Drew," she announced. The back of Reid's head was visible over the sofa and a war movie was on the screen—her least favorite.

"Reid?"

She rounded the couch to find him slumped, eyes closed, a half-empty bottle of Jack Daniel's in one hand. She reached for the bottle before he spilled liquor on the couch, and he jerked awake.

"What the hell!" he barked. His eyes were dark with fury, his mouth a hateful tilt.

"Are you… What happened to you tonight?"

He avoided looking her in the eye. "You're in my way," he growled. "What the bloody hell are you doing here, anyway?"

Okay, she had no idea what was with his Jekyll/Hyde behavior, but she wasn't going to stand here and take it. He'd never talked to her this way. She snatched away the remote and flicked off the TV.

"Hand it over!" He tried to stand but he stumbled, crashing onto the couch in an inelegant heap.

"Give me the bottle and I'll give you the remote."

"No deal." He took another swig, spilling whiskey over his chin before setting aside the bottle.

"I waited for you for over two hours," she told him. "And you were here the whole time…getting drunk?"

"It's *my* birthday."

"I thought you wanted to spend it with—" *someone you love* "—me."

A flash of guilt lit his expression and vanished just as fast. "Yeah, well."

"Why didn't you call me? Or answer my text?" Things couldn't end this way. She wouldn't *let them* end this way. "At the very least, I'm owed the respect of a reply."

"With a heart emoji," he slurred, glowering up at her.

There it was. Her fear confirmed. She'd convinced

herself on the way over here that she'd been overreacting. He had held that stupid red heart emoji against her.

"I—"

"Get out, Drew." Those words were spoken plainly, not an iota of a slur or hesitation, which made them all the harder to hear. He pointed to the door. "Before I call security."

"I am not going to let you kick me out of here without an explanation."

"Yes, you are." This time he did stand, bearing down on her with nostrils flared. "You'll do it because I asked. And because you deserve better than someone who can't be who you need. You deserve someone who texts hearts back to you… Someone who shows up. Someone without all this baggage." Pain crept into Reid's eyes. "You deserve someone—" he touched her cheek gently "—better than me."

His eyes fluttered, and he swayed, nearly toppling over. She grabbed his arms and—thank God for the trainers at the gym—was able to reroute him to the couch, where he fell with a *whump*. He lay on his left shoulder, awkwardly positioned, eyes shut. A soft snore came next.

There was something else going on with him— something bigger than heart emojis and birthday dinners. Maybe he'd gotten a call from his father that his mother wasn't okay, or maybe he'd called his mum for support and she hadn't offered any.

No matter what had happened, Drew couldn't leave him here alone. She'd never seen Reid behave this way. She couldn't be certain that he was in his right mind, or that he wouldn't attempt to drive somewhere. Someone had to stay with him and make sure he was okay, and that someone couldn't be her. Reid didn't want her here. He'd made that clear.

But she knew who could help. The same person she'd always turned to first whenever she'd been in trouble. After the second ring, her brother answered.

"Hey, sis."

"Gage," she spoke around a lump in her throat, frightened and worried now that the anger had passed. "I need you to come to Reid's."

Twenty-Three

Tate had drunk enough wine at his birthday celebration to tranquilize a grizzly bear, but apparently it hadn't been enough to keep him asleep through the night.

He bolted upright, his chest heaving. A sheen of cold sweat covered him, and his head throbbed like hell.

He was momentarily disoriented by the pale blue walls and the pink floral comforter, the whitewashed dresser that glowed in the moonlight streaming in through the window. Then he remembered he was at Claire's apartment. She'd driven him here after the restaurant where Tate had wine. Like, *all* the wine.

His fiancée was fast asleep, her perfect bone structure aglow and her neatly brushed blond hair fanning over the pillow.

He touched her gently, half expecting her to turn into smoke and vanish altogether. That's the way he'd felt ever since the phone call with his mother yesterday. As if his entire life had been a mirage. She'd said they needed to talk, and that hadn't been the half of it...

"We need to talk."

"Then talk."

"Not over the phone. Plus, your father will want to be there."

"Don't do this to me, dammit." He'd never spoken to his mother that way his whole life, but desperate times... *"I'm sorry. I can't... You have to tell me something, Mom. I feel like I'm losing my mind."*

She sighed, a ragged sound from the depths. Frankly, he was terrified what she'd say next.

"Everything your father and I have told you about your past, your parentage and your childhood is true."

Tate released the breath he was holding. The back of his head hit the headrest in relief. "Thank God."

But before he could completely relax, his mother added, "As far as we know."

When she'd started to cry, he'd known something was severely off. She refused to tell him any more over the phone. He'd boarded the ferry and returned to Spright Island. But even his sanctuary within the luxury wellness community he ran and operated wasn't enough to lift the weight of dread from his shoulders.

His parents had traveled to his house to talk to him

in person this morning, and what they'd told him was at once better and worse than Tate had imagined.

He ran through the list of what he now knew for sure.

One, he was adopted at age three.

He pictured Reid in the café. *Our third birthday party was a circus theme...*

Two, he was born to British parents, which was why he used to have an accent.

You're Wesley Singleton and you were born in London.

And finally, the new information that had come to light: his parents had always been suspicious of the agency from where they'd adopted Tate.

"We fell in love with you on sight," his mother had said through heaving sobs as she stood in his living room.

His father hadn't been crying, but his throat had been choked with emotion when he admitted that he, too, had been suspicious. *"But we never doubted your parents were dead. We knew it was unscrupulous for the agency to ask for an extra fee, but we loved you so very much."*

They'd paid over $100,000 in "processing fees" to rush the adoption process. The agency had provided the death certificates of Tate's alleged birth parents, and that had been the end of their communication with the agency.

"We *still* love you so much," his mother had said.

Tate loved them, too, but hadn't been able to return the sentiment at that moment. Instead, he'd given them his spare key and invited them to stay at his home on Spright Island for a while.

He'd returned to Seattle to Claire, arriving about six hours earlier than he'd planned and with a packed bag. Then he'd pasted on a smile as fake as he suspected those death certificates were and told her he missed her.

They'd been dating a little over a year, and he'd proposed a month ago. They hadn't decided yet where to live, though it made more sense to him to stay in Spright Island since he owned a home there and Claire rented. They'd tabled the discussion for the time being. To think he'd believed her hesitation was the biggest cause for turmoil in his otherwise worry-free life.

Worry-free until now.

He'd spent the day and evening with Claire and two couples who had started out as friends of hers. Tate hadn't enjoyed the dinner or the company, or even the wine. He'd used the substance to numb himself.

He'd kept what his parents told him secret and vowed to keep it secret until the day he *actually* died. No good could come from rocking the boat. None at all.

Claire made a soft noise and touched his arm.

"Okay?" she murmured, her eyes closed.

"Yeah. Fine." He bent and kissed her smooth cheek and slid out of bed. "Just hungry," he lied.

In the kitchen he stood with a bottle of water and stared at the black sky, at the barely visible stars struggling to twinkle through the light pollution of the city.

Somewhere out there was a man named Reid Singleton who believed that Tate was his brother. Who believed that Tate was named *Wesley*.

"And that I was kidnapped by a circus clown," he said aloud with a hoarse chuckle. The laugh died on his lips as a vision flashed on the screen of his mind.

No, not a vision.

A memory.

A memory of a little boy with the same color eyes as him snatching a stuffed Curious George toy and throwing it into a swimming pool.

Then another vision attacked like virtual reality— he could practically feel the large, rough hands that caught him under the armpits. Smell gasoline on the fingers that had covered his mouth.

And as three-year-old Tate had been carried into the woods, he saw a blur of bright colors—a red-and-yellow inflatable where kids played in a sea of plastic blue and green balls—against a brown cottage in a lush yard.

Home.

The word hit him with such a certainty that his knees weakened. The pounding in his head dialed up to ten. He sank to his ass on Claire's mahogany wood flooring, no longer able to find the strength to stand.

It was real.

Everything Reid had said.

"My brother," he whispered to the dark room.

"Tate?" Claire, wrapping a short silk robe over

her lithe frame, padded out into the kitchen. "Are you okay?".

"I'm not Tate." He smiled up at his fiancée but his mind was in a sad, distant place. "My name is Wesley," he told her in as good a British accent as he could muster.

Twenty-Four

When Drew heard the light rap at the front door, she was next to it, having waited for her brother to arrive in the foyer rather than watch over Reid. First off, he was fine—drunk, sure, but fine. At least physically. Second, she was still pretty angry with him, and standing over him fuming wasn't productive.

She pulled open Reid's front door and Gage scanned her red dress and heels darkly. "Where is he?"

"Passed out on the couch."

Gage stalked past her. In the living room, he took inventory of Reid's position before bending over and hauling his best friend into a sitting position.

Drew stood off to the side as Gage slapped Reid's face—not hard enough to rattle his teeth but hard enough that Reid's eyes rolled open.

Reid threw himself forward and squeezed Gage into a hug. "Wesley."

Gage peeled his friend off his shoulders. "Reid. Man. What is going on with you?"

"Gage?" Reid blinked a few times, his eyes damp with tears. "I thought you were my brother."

His brother? Ho boy. She'd been right. Something was going on with him that had nothing to do with her.

"It's our birthday."

"I know it's your birthday."

"*Our* birthday. I stood up Drew." Reid sent her a glare. "She won't leave."

Gage's jaw tightened, and he slid a withering glare Drew's way. Then he told his friend, "You are going to owe her a really big thank-you in the morning for putting up with your shit." He pulled Reid up by the shoulders, wrapped one arm around him and dragged him into the bedroom.

Drew lifted her purse from the barstool in the kitchen and tiptoed toward the front door.

"Sit your ass down." Gage bypassed her to go to the fridge and grab a bottle of water. "Give me thirty seconds."

She wanted to tell him she didn't owe him an explanation, but she did. They'd always been close. She confided in her brother about everything. Hell, he was the one she called when her heart was broken. Him, not a girlfriend. Gage always knew what to say to make it better, and she trusted him not to spill her secrets to anyone—especially Mom and Dad. And right now her heart was definitely broken.

She dropped her purse on the kitchen counter and sat on the barstool, her chin in her hands while she waited for Gage's return.

He arrived a minute later and pulled two bottles of beer from Reid's fridge. Uncapping them, he watched her with a look of disappointment—which was worse than if he'd been angry.

"Him, I'll take to task when he's good and hungover." Gage took a long guzzle of beer, and she did the same. "You, I'm dealing with now." He leaned on the counter. "What's going on, Drew?"

"Reid and I have been…seeing each other."

"You mean sleeping together."

She winced. "Yeah."

Gage shut his eyes slowly, took a deep breath, and after steeling himself, nodded. "Go on."

She told him about California and about Reid not recognizing her.

She told him about the crush she'd had when she was younger. She told him how Reid had come to mean more to her than she'd expected. How it was her idea that they not tell Gage. Then she told him that Reid never dated Christina. How Drew planned his birthday party because Reid told her a big secret about why his birthday was such an unhappy time of year.

"Why?"

She averted her eyes. "I can't tell you that."

"Yes, you can."

"I really can't." She picked the label on the beer bottle with her thumbnail. "It's something you're going to have to hear from Reid himself. I promised."

Her brother nodded, but still didn't seem happy about…well, any of it. "You're in love with him, aren't you?"

She nodded, and a tear spilled down her cheek.

Gage pulled her into a tight hug. "Why'd you do that?"

"I don't know," she sobbed. "I thought he'd want to make this last a little longer. I was going to tell him how I felt tonight."

"Shh-shh. Listen." He held her face in his hands and gave her a soft smile. "Try not to worry, okay? I'm going to stay here. I'll talk to him. I'll find out why he was such a dick to you earlier. No matter what big secret he has, Drew, you know you deserve more than what he's offering."

"Funny. That's what he said to me." She offered a watery smile. "I thought I'd change his mind. That he'd see how great we are together. How good I am for him."

"This doesn't have anything to do with you. If anything, you're too good for him." Gage kissed her forehead. "You okay to drive home?"

"Completely sober," she said instead, because she wasn't okay. Not even a little. But she took her brother's advice and left. The only other option was to stay here, and she sure as hell wasn't doing that.

At home, Drew kicked off her shoes and crawled into bed, still wearing her red dress. She was exhausted from the taxing emotions of the day. The last thing she thought about before sleep took hold were Reid's words to Gage.

I thought you were my brother.

What was that about?

The second cup of coffee was helping. He hoped.

Reid hovered over his half-empty mug, cupping his aching head in both hands. It was like a nuclear bomb had gone off in his skull. Gage stood sentinel at the countertop, arms folded over his chest. He'd been like that all morning. He hadn't done a damn thing to help Reid get over his hangover, either. He'd started off by coming into Reid's room and clapping his hands together while yelling, "Time to get up!" over and over.

Reid had dragged his aching carcass into the shower and emerged feeling not much better. In his kitchen, Gage stood, mug of coffee in hand, and when Reid asked for one he poured the entire pot down the drain.

So much for best friends.

Reid had made another pot of coffee and poured himself a cup while Gage made himself a plate of scrambled eggs. He ate, and Reid refilled his coffee mug. And that's when Gage decided to speak.

"Talk, Singleton. Why are you messing with Drew?"

"I'm not messing with her."

"But you are fucking her."

"Do you want your ass kicked?" Reid barked, adrenaline pouring through his veins like hot lava.

"That's my line."

He'd never seen his friend this pissed off before. Gage had every right. Reid was in the wrong pursuing Drew and hadn't treated her well last night. He hadn't been able to reconcile having a birthday now that he knew his brother was alive and well and in the same damn city. After a night and day of emotional upheaval was it any wonder he'd turned to whiskey for a reprieve? His thoughts had been an unsortable mess since he'd found Wesley returned from the dead, and then lost him all over again.

Reid wouldn't have been good company at Drew's soft opening anyhow. Yes, he should've contacted her, but what the hell would he have said? *Sorry, too drunk to show up after finding my brother alive*. He had no idea how to tell her what he'd learned…how to tell anyone.

"My life took a complicated turn last night," Reid mumbled.

"What's so complicated?" Gage pressed. "You can't sort your heart from your dick? So you slept with my sister until she got in too deep and now you're punishing her for liking you too much?"

"No. That's not—this isn't about Drew." Reid palmed his head. It ached 5 percent less than when he woke up this morning, which was a crowning achievement. His pending breakdown was far more than Drew had signed up for. If she thought he'd had baggage before, it was nothing compared to the entire airport's worth he had now.

"I'm trying to protect her," Reid told Gage, but the excuse sounded lame even to his own ears.

Gage narrowed his eyelids. "That's my job."

"I…" Reid swallowed thickly, worried that Gage would think him bonkers once he told him about Tate. Worried more that Gage would write him off completely when he found out that Drew wasn't the only secret Reid had kept from him over the years. But Reid owed him an explanation, not to save his own hide but because Gage was his oldest friend.

"I have a twin brother," he said. "And up until two days ago I thought he was dead." Reid told him about the birthday party that ended up being a search party and everything else leading up until now. How his parents had never handled the day well. How Reid hadn't celebrated a birthday since.

While he spoke, Gage's face grew pale.

"I was in Brewdog's for coffee and, Gage, I swear as I sit here he was right behind me in line."

"How?"

"I have no idea. I told him who he was. He didn't believe me. He introduced himself as Tate Duncan from California. But he had a scar I recognized. He has my eyes. It was my brother, Wesley. I'd know him anywhere." A fresh wave of pain zapped his chest. "He threw away my card. He didn't believe me," he repeated numbly.

"Reid… I… And now? Do you still believe that was Wesley?"

"With everything I am." Reid shoved his coffee away, his stomach on fire. "I might be more certain than before."

"And you didn't tell Drew about him?"

"I told her about his death, but I didn't tell her I saw him." Reid blinked in shock. "That he wasn't dead." He blinked up at Gage. "I was processing."

"You were processing," Gage bit out. "Not only have you been keeping the relationship between you and Drew from me, but you've been keeping this secret, as well? From me, from Flynn and Sabrina? We've been friends for years, Reid. You could've told us."

"I know." Reid hung his pounding head.

"Drew would've understood."

Reid was beginning the suspect Gage was right. But finding his brother was alive hadn't changed who Reid was—he hadn't suddenly become whole. In fact, he felt more broken than ever. "Drew and I were supposed to break up this month, anyway. Last night seemed apt."

"Did you really think she would let you go after she was with you for nearly *two months*?"

When Gage put it that way, it made Reid feel daft. Of course she wouldn't shrug their time off together. She was different, and with her, Reid had been different.

Gage shook his head pitiably. "Lucky for you I fell in love with someone who wasn't honest about her identity at first, either. I have a high tolerance for understanding."

"You thought she was a man," Reid teased. Andy's website hadn't featured her photo so they'd assumed by name and reputation alone that she was a male. What a bunch of sexist bastards they'd been. "Until we laid eyes on her, we all thought that."

Gage smiled, unable to keep a stone face when his fiancée was mentioned. He refilled his coffee mug, topping off Reid's as well—a good sign Reid was on his way to being forgiven. "How have you not tracked this Tate guy down yet?"

"I used to search online for him once I was old enough to know what I was doing. Just in case we'd been mistaken. I researched adoption agencies, missing children reports. I finally gave up. Accepted the inevitable. That casket was empty, but Wesley may as well have been inside it. He was a ghost."

"A ghost who has returned." Gage raised his eyebrows. "And now you know his name and where he's from."

"I do." Hope dawned, sharp and bold. He knew enough to track him down.

"We'll call every Duncan household in California," Gage said as he lifted his phone to his ear. "Every Tate Duncan in the Pacific Northwest."

"Who're you calling?"

"We need help." Then into the phone, Gage said, "Flynn. Can you and Sabrina come to Reid's? Yes. Now."

Twenty-Five

It was hard to mourn Reid when she wasn't sure they'd ever had anything to begin with. Drew wasn't even sure they were broken up.

Reid was gone. That much she knew.

Gage had called her late on Sunday to tell her... well, not much. She knew that Reid woke with a killer hangover, that Flynn and Sabrina and Gage had spent the day together. That they all knew Reid's secret about his twin brother going missing when Reid was three years old, and about the funeral when Reid was eight.

What she didn't know was what had driven Reid to drown his sorrows in whiskey and treat her like she'd never mattered. She'd told Gage as much and he'd given her the best big-brother speech ever.

"It's inexcusable the way he talked to you that night and I'm sorry," Gage had said. "I love you so much. I'm trying to be there for him, but trust me, I'm on your side. If he doesn't make some sort of amends with you soon, I'm not sure we'll be friends much longer. I choose you, kiddo."

She'd burst into tears and cried on her phone's screen, telling Gage that she was at fault as well, and that he shouldn't leave his best friend for her. She should've told Reid how she felt about him a long time ago. She'd dreamed up the plan for a perfect evening when, really, wouldn't a simple heart-to-heart have been enough?

"He has a lot to make up for with all of us," Gage had said, sounding as hollow as she felt.

It seemed everyone was in a holding pattern while Reid was in London. She didn't know why he was there, but assumed he was trying to find some closure with his family. She didn't know why this birthday in particular had been a trigger for him, but there was more to the story that she didn't know about. Gage let on that he knew, but refused to tell her, even though she'd begged.

"I can't, Drew. The same way you knew I had to hear from Reid, you are going to have to hear this from Reid, too. He swore all of us to secrecy, saying he had to sort it out for himself. We owe him that."

"It's that big, huh?" she'd asked, acceptance an arrow through her heart.

"Yes. It is."

So that was that. Reid was in London and she was

in Seattle and had no idea when he'd be back, why he'd gone there or if he'd ever speak to her again.

As much as it'd hurt to do it she'd deleted his phone number and text messages from her phone. She needed a clean break. Seeing that damn heart emoji in her text messages only reminded her of the worst night of her life. She needed to pull on her big-girl panties and remember who she'd become.

A woman who was building a career without the support or help of a man. Reid was no Devin Briggs, but somehow he'd managed to hurt her more than Devin, and in a much shorter span of time.

She hated Reid for that as much as she loved him in spite of it. It would be a long road, but she wasn't going to lie around in wait for him to come to some conclusion about them. Good God, it'd taken him a decade to tell his best friends about his loss. How long would he keep her in the dark about this new turn of events?

"Hey, Drew." She turned to find Beaux, the bartender, a bottle of white wine in hand. Fig & Truffle, the Market location, was opening tonight, and she was ready. They all were. "Do we have more chardonnay?"

"Let me check." She walked past him, but he caught her arm gently, his blond eyebrows lowering in concern.

"You're better off without him." Beaux nodded resolutely, and she forced a grin. He'd been there the night of the failed birthday dinner. It wasn't much of a leap to put Reid's absence together with her sadness and arrive at the logical conclusion she'd been dumped.

"You're absolutely right. I'll check on the chardonnay." Keys in hand, she walked to the wine cellar as the cliché Beaux offered echoed in her mind. She didn't believe she'd be better off without Reid, but she had to believe that to make it through tonight. And the next night. And the night after that.

However long it took for her heart to heal after being torn apart.

Reid had been in London for nearly two weeks. He'd gone to his parents' home to stay, and they'd been delighted to see him. It was rare he popped in for a surprise visit. Hell, he'd never popped in for a surprise visit.

As glad as they were to see him, however, he couldn't feel good about being here. He had news for them he knew wouldn't be welcome.

And he'd put it off for too long.

He'd played off the extended visit as "old home week," and he'd made good on that bargain as well, hunting down old friends and cousins he'd not seen in years. He'd spent a lot of time at the pub—every damned night. Last night he and his father had downed their fair share of scotch while sitting at the fire. Mum had long since gone to bed, and the scotch warm in his veins, Reid found it the perfect time to tell his father what had happened in Seattle.

George Singleton had taken the news well. Stoically, actually. The tremor in his hand had rattled his half-empty glass, but he'd listened intently as Reid caught him up.

Flynn was the one who'd called the correct Tate Duncan. He'd reached him via Spright Island's realty office. A woman named Shelley had answered the phone. Flynn had convinced her that he and Tate had met up in Seattle, but he'd lost Tate's number and was interested in bringing more business to their community. She'd mentioned that Tate had taken the week off. "I believe he's in Seattle now at his fiancée's house," Shelley had said. "Would you like me to leave him a message to call you?"

"It's urgent. So, yes." Flynn had relayed Reid's phone number. "If you could give him the name Reid Singleton and tell him it's an emergency. He'll understand."

Flynn had ended the call and nodded to the four of them seated at Reid's kitchen table, each in front of their own laptops. "I think that was him."

Sabrina had reached for Reid's hand, and he'd held on to her tightly, feeling as if his friends were the only thing keeping him bolted to the earth. Like without them he'd go hurtling into space until the oxygen was robbed of his body and he collapsed like a meaningless black hole.

Reid sat across from his mother at the breakfast table now, who was wholly ignoring her sausage and eggs. His father held her hand, his expression unreadable. She cried softly, and Reid wanted to stop talking. To stop breaking her heart into tiny pieces. Unfortunately, there was more to tell her.

No going back now.

"Wes—Tate Duncan called me, Mum. That afternoon. Within an hour of Flynn's phone call, he called me back." He drew in a deep breath as his mother's face filled with hope. "He's…not ready. To meet either of you."

She collapsed into his father's arms, her wailing sobs drawing wetness to Reid's own eyes. George shushed his wife and rubbed her shoulders, there for her when she needed him most.

Exactly the opposite of Reid's reaction to Drew, and he'd needed her even more than she'd needed him.

Reid hadn't been able to lean on her even when he'd received the knee-weakening call from his brother. The one where Wesley plainly stated that he'd remembered being snatched.

"Must've been a repressed memory or something." Tate's voice was low, his tone flat. Reid remained silent. *"I spoke with my parents. My adoptive parents. They told me something I've never known before. The agency that facilitated the adoption was…sketchy. They extorted money from them. A lot of it. My mom said she was too in love with me to see the truth for what it was. That the death certificates for my birth parents could've been faked."*

It was a lot to take in—then and now. It was so much that Reid didn't say any more to his mother about what Tate had relayed to him about the adoption. But there was a sliver of hope he could give her, and thank God for that.

"I need to tell you some good news." Reid patted her arm and his mother—his beautiful mother with her stylish gray hair and trim figure, and green-blue eyes—pulled her face from George's neck to fasten Reid with a look that conveyed so much hope his heart broke for her.

"He's agreed to meet me for dinner when I go home. It's a start at building a relationship. He has a lot to sort out. And so do we." Reid wasn't sure how he'd handle a man he didn't know coming up to him in a coffee shop and saying he was his long-lost twin brother. He supposed he'd have become angry and stormed out, like Wesley had. How did anyone even begin to accept their entire life was a lie?

"I promise you both," Reid told his parents, "that I will do everything in my power to bring him to meet you."

"Or us to meet him." Jane wiped away her tears and offered a brittle smile. "We will fly to Washington, darling. We will."

"I know you will. And as soon as I navigate around this very sensitive subject of Wes—Tate accepting that we're his family, I will put you on a plane myself. But keep your hopes in check. Just in case."

She nodded excitedly, and he could see that her hopes were most certainly not in check.

"Can we call him?" she asked.

"I don't know. But you can call me." He held his mother's hand. "You can call me and I'll tell you everything about him and how our dinner went. And

I will tell him that it's best for all of us if we reunite as soon as possible."

Jane's tender smile was like the sun bursting through dark clouds. "My baby boy."

Reid assumed she was referring to Wesley until she moved from George's embrace and into Reid's. He held his mother as she cried against him and vowed that no matter what, he'd make that reunion happen. If it took him the rest of his mother's life to convince Wesley to reunite with his actual family, Reid wouldn't give up on his twin brother.

Not ever, ever again.

"There's more I have to tell you," he told his mother as she calmed. He smoothed his hand along her back. "I've met someone."

Jane pulled herself from his arms, her face a comical expression of shock. She didn't know details about his love life, but she knew he wasn't one to settle down. "Have you?"

"*The* one."

He was as sure of it as he was sure that Tate Duncan was Wesley Singleton. He was as sure of Drew being his destiny as he was the sun would rise in the east. He was sure, for the first time in his life, that the pieces of his life had intersected at this precise moment for a reason.

Drew was meant to be his.

"She's my best mate's sister. Her name is Drew. And she's the most beautiful woman in the world." He tapped his mother's chin. "Save you."

A crack of laughter sounded from his mother—

possibly the best sound he'd ever heard. "Well, where is she then?"

"She's at home. And I need to tell her what I've learned. About Wesley and about myself." Reid had believed himself incapable of loving or trusting anyone. He'd believed that his running into Tate was a premonition of danger; a warning to turn back. He'd reasoned that he was leaving for Drew because she deserved to be with someone who wasn't a train wreck waiting to happen.

But as these two weeks had passed he'd realized the train wreck had already happened and Drew hadn't hesitated to sift through the wreckage and find the surviving parts of his heart. Of his very *soul*.

She'd been everything to him before he'd been brave enough to admit it, and now that his life was more unstable than ever, he knew she was his port in the storm.

She was his home.

"I hope she'll take me back," he said to his parents, but mostly to himself. His eyes on his empty breakfast plate he added, "And I hope she believes me when I tell her how much I love her."

Twenty-Six

Drew helped Christina unload her bags from the trunk. Her flight left in an hour, so she needed to hustle. "Have a safe—*oof*!"

Christina hugged Drew tightly, practically choking her in the process. "I'm a horrible, awful, terrible person!"

"Can't...breathe." Drew tapped her roommate's shoulders insistently, half kidding, half needing Chris to release the boa constrictor hold on her neck.

"Oh. Sorry."

Drew inhaled melodramatically before offering her friend a wink. "You're a wonderful, sweet, loving person."

"You shouldn't be consoling me! I'm taking a job

in Chicago with almost no notice and leaving you here to fend for yourself at the worst possible time."

"You're taking your dream job," Drew corrected, ignoring the "worst possible time" thing. It'd been over two weeks since she'd heard from Reid, which had sucked her soul into an emotionless vacuum, but she couldn't pin that on Christina. "You paid me rent for the remainder of this month and next, what more could I ask of you? I'm planning on paying you back, by the way—"

"No, you're not. My signing bonus was huge. I want you to have it because I love you." Christina grinned. "I'm going to miss you." They hugged again.

"You're also going to miss your dream flight to your dream job if you don't get going."

Christina dragged her wheeled suitcase behind her and blew Drew a kiss. "I'll call you when I'm settled!"

"You'd better!"

Christina vanished behind the reflective glass doors of the airport terminal, and Drew buckled herself up in the driver's seat. It was the end of an era. Christina hadn't been shy about telling Drew she'd had an eye on Downey Design for her entire adult life. Every time she'd consider applying, though, she'd reasoned her way out of it. Chris didn't know anything about Chicago, didn't want to make new friends, blah, blah, blah. Then that day she'd lain on the sofa while Drew was sharing her first drink with Reid in California, Christina had been brave enough to upload her portfolio.

They'd responded last week and asked her to start right away.

Drew was happy for her friend. Almost as happy for her as she was miserable for herself.

Lately, Gage and Andy had stuck to Drew like a dryer sheet. She could scarcely find a moment to herself if she wasn't at work. Either Andy wanted to take her to lunch or out shopping, or Gage was fussing over repairs in her apartment. He'd come over to change light bulbs for her yesterday—as if she couldn't have done that herself?

She appreciated his doting, though. It showed that Gage loved her, and Andy did, too. So did Christina.

Everyone loves me except the man I want to love me most of all.

What a miserable reminder that was. *Thanks a lot, Brain.*

No problem.

Sundays used to be her favorite day, but now Drew resented the spare time. Gage and Andy weren't hovering since they knew Drew was driving Christina to the airport, and with both of them working full-time jobs, they had to make the most of the weekends. And what more could they do for Drew? She was sad, and there wasn't any fixing it.

Except for...

She cut that thought off at the knees.

The grill marks on the halibut were perfection. The red and green sauces the perfect yin-yang design on the square white plate. Drew rested the piece of fish in the center, sprinkled it with smoked, flaked sea salt and then balanced a small tuft of microgreens atop the fish.

She'd been trying to perfect this dish for quite some time, and now the dish was as pleasing to the eye as she knew it tasted. But just to make sure...

She grabbed a fork and lifted a bite to her lips. A sharp knock came from her front door and, her mouth watering, she sent a forlorn look at the fish.

"I knew you couldn't stay away," she called to what had to be Andy or Gage—or both of them. She turned the knob and pulled, then froze solid at the sight of the man standing in her doorway with a bouquet of roses.

Red roses.

"My brother's alive," Reid said.

Drew blinked as she processed that news. "I don't understand."

"I know. Can I come in?"

"I don't think that's a good idea." As wonderful as it was to see Reid's ridiculously handsome face, she was also feeling pretty damned protective over her own heart. How could she and Reid ever make it if he didn't trust her enough to tell her what was happening in his life? "I ran into him the day before my birthday," Reid continued from the entryway. "At Brewdog's. I bought him a cup of coffee and then blurted out that his name wasn't Tate Duncan like he thought it was. I told him he was Wesley Singleton and scared the life out of him. He thought I was scamming him or something. Anyway. I found him.

He remembers being kidnapped. Not much around it or after it, but he remembers the birthday party. He remembers our childhood home in London. And he remembers me."

It was a lot of information to take in, but while Reid talked, her broken heart took a back seat to the miracle that had occurred.

She couldn't hide her awe. "That's incredible."

"He's living outside of Seattle. On an island you have to take the ferry to get to. We're having dinner this Friday, and I'm almost as sick over it as I am excited."

"It's the best news." She found herself returning Reid's infectious smile.

"It is. It truly is. And I didn't share it with you." His smile fell. "I have more I want to say if I could give you these—" he held up the flowers "—and come inside. If you want me gone, I'll leave. If after you hear me out you can't forgive me and have nothing left for me, I will leave, Drew. I promise. But if what I say changes everything…it'd be worth it to both of us for you to hear me out."

She watched him for several seconds. He was in dark gray jeans and a weathered T-shirt. He was holding six red roses, and the expression on his face was as sincere as she'd ever seen. As much as he'd hurt her—as much as she'd been hurting—she couldn't deny herself the chance to hear what he'd come here to tell her.

She stepped aside and he walked in, resting the

roses on the kitchen table. "I've interrupted your dinner. It's a work of art."

"It's perfect," she said. "And probably the only perfect thing left in my life. That's your fault."

"I know it is. And finding Wes—Tate…" He pinched the bridge of his nose, and she felt for him, she really did. He had to be struggling with finding his brother, with adjusting to him being alive and potentially a part of his life again. She wondered how his parents had reacted. They had to be overjoyed. After decades, their family was whole again.

But you're not, she reminded herself.

As great as the news was that Reid's twin brother was alive, there was unfinished business between Reid and her. She deserved an apology. Thankfully, he knew just where to start.

"I'm sorry I shut you out, Drew. I'm absolute shit at sharing with the people in my life. I could argue it was because of losing my brother at such an early age. I could explain that being a twin feels like you're half of a whole, and I haven't been whole in a long time. But I should've trusted you. I should've come to you. I should never have stood you up without a word of explanation." He sighed, his eyebrows bending in remorse. "I never should have been so cruel to you when you came to my apartment. You were concerned and I… I was a complete wreck."

He stepped closer but didn't touch her. She wasn't sure if she wanted him to or not. She had no idea if he'd simply come here to make reparations and then leave things as is, or if there was more. Then he cleared that up for her, too.

"I want you, Drew Fleming. Not only in my bed, but in my life. You have a way of pushing me into realms I'd have never discovered on my own. You're healing the deepest part of me. The part that has never been whole. I tried handling this on my own. I tried to clean up the mess and not involve you, but…"

He paused as if gathering his courage, and then started again. "I need you. I have long prided myself on never needing anyone, but you…you're different. I love you in a way I've never loved anyone before. I don't want you at arm's length. I want to come home to you and I want to be held by you when I've had a shit day. I've never thought myself a family man, but when I picture our lives—our marriage and our children—with my family, with my brother, I can hardly breathe because the joy is too great."

Her eyes filled with tears. The picture he painted bloomed to life inside her head with hardly any effort. Marriage, a beautiful baby boy in her arms, celebrating Christmas in London…

"I screwed up. I have no excuse for being a complete wanker. But I can absolutely promise you that I won't do it again. I won't shut you out of my life, and I won't ever keep secrets. I love you too much to risk losing you again." He swallowed thickly, his Adam's apple bobbing. "If you can accept my apology and let me try again, I promise I'm worth loving. If you can let yourself love me."

"I already let myself love you, Reid. It's what I was

going to tell you on your birthday. I was planning on telling you how I felt that night." She felt the loss of that night fresh. "I thought once you saw what I'd planned for you, once you were there with the gold and black streamers and the perfect steak dinner…" It sounded so foolish now that she said it out loud. "I don't know what I was thinking. I should've just told you how I felt."

"Streamers?" Realization dawned on Reid's face. "That night…there wasn't a soft opening, was there?" he asked miserably.

"It was a birthday dinner for you. A private one. I borrowed the Fig & Truffle and hired a server, bartender and chef. I wanted you to have a good birthday memory to add to the bad ones. I knew it wouldn't make up for what you'd lost, but I thought it might soften the blow."

Reid stood stock-still and simply stared. "Wow. I really don't deserve you."

"No. Probably not."

"I'm sorry. For all of it." His mouth turned down at the corners. "That was my piece. I've said it. Have I earned my second chance?"

She rested one hand on his cheek and peered up at the beautiful, lost dope of a man who couldn't trust his own heart or himself when he'd finally found true love. "You're still on your *first* chance. I'm completely and totally in love with you. I want marriage and kids and I want to go to London."

His smile emerged, followed by a laugh that sounded suspiciously emotional.

"You're the man for me, and I knew it from the first second I laid eyes on your gorgeous face. It just took us both time to find ourselves. To grow into the people who were right for each other."

"Please, Drew. Can I kiss you and make it all right?"

She looped her arms around his neck and breathed in the leather scent of his cologne. She was home in his arms and he in hers. They would get through this the way they were meant to go through everything in life: *together.*

Against his lips, she whispered, "You'd better do more than kiss me, Reid Singleton."

* * * * *

Don't miss Reid's twin brother Tate's story coming October 2019 from Harlequin Desire!

Tate Duncan's stable life has been upended. He's lost a fiancée and gained an entirely new family. Christmas in London with strangers isn't something he's willing to do alone—enter Hayden Green, Spright Island's yoga instructor and Tate's saving grace. She agrees to stand in as his fiancée and accompany him on the trip of a lifetime, never suspecting that she might lose her heart in the process...

COMING NEXT MONTH FROM

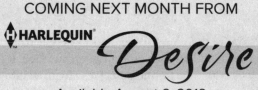

HARLEQUIN®

Desire

Available August 6, 2019

#2677 BIG SHOT
by Katy Evans
Dealing with her insufferable hotshot boss has India Crowley at the breaking point. But when he faces a stand-in daddy dilemma, India can't deny him a helping hand. Sharing close quarters, though, may mean facing her true feelings about the man...

#2678 OFF LIMITS LOVERS
Texas Cattleman's Club: Houston • by Reese Ryan
When attorney Roarke Perry encounters the daughter of his father's arch enemy, he's dumbstruck. Annabel Currin is irresistible—and she desperately needs his help. Yet keeping this gorgeous client at arms' length may prove impossible once forbidden feelings take over!

#2679 REDEEMED BY PASSION
Dynasties: Secrets of the A-List • by Joss Wood
Event planner Teresa St. Clair is organizing the wedding of the year so she can help her brother out of a dangerous debt. She doesn't need meddling—or saving—from her ex, gorgeous billionaire Liam Christopher. But she can't seem to stay away...

#2680 MONTANA SEDUCTION
Two Brothers • by Jules Bennett
Dane Michaels will stop at nothing to get the Montana resort that rightfully belongs to him and his brother. Even if it means getting close to his rival's daughter. As long as he doesn't fall for the very woman he's seducing...

#2681 HIS MARRIAGE DEMAND
The Stewart Heirs • by Yahrah St. John
With her family business going under, CEO Fallon Stewart needs a miracle. But Gage Campbell, the newly wealthy man she betrayed as a teen, has a bailout plan...if Fallon will pose as his wife! Can she keep focused as passion takes over their mock marriage?

#2682 FROM RICHES TO REDEMPTION
Switched! • by Andrea Laurence
Ten years ago, River Atkinson and Morgan Steele eloped, but the heiress's father tore them apart. Now, just as Morgan's very identity is called into question, River is back in town. Will secrets sidetrack their second chance, or are they on the road to redemption?

YOU CAN FIND MORE INFORMATION ON UPCOMING HARLEQUIN® TITLES, FREE EXCERPTS AND MORE AT WWW.HARLEQUIN.COM.

HDCNM0719

Get 4 FREE REWARDS!

We'll send you 2 FREE Books
plus 2 FREE Mystery Gifts.

Harlequin® Desire books feature heroes who have it all: wealth, status, incredible good looks... everything but the right woman.

FREE
Value Over
$20

YES! Please send me 2 FREE Harlequin® Desire novels and my 2 FREE gifts (gifts are worth about $10 retail). After receiving them, if I don't wish to receive any more books, I can return the shipping statement marked "cancel." If I don't cancel, I will receive 6 brand-new novels every month and be billed just $4.55 per book in the U.S. or $5.24 per book in Canada. That's a savings of at least 13% off the cover price! It's quite a bargain! Shipping and handling is just 50¢ per book in the U.S. and $1.25 per book in Canada.* I understand that accepting the 2 free books and gifts places me under no obligation to buy anything. I can always return a shipment and cancel at any time. The free books and gifts are mine to keep no matter what I decide.

225/326 HDN GNND

Name (please print)

Address   Apt. #

City   State/Province   Zip/Postal Code

Mail to the **Reader Service:**
IN U.S.A.: P.O. Box 1341, Buffalo, NY 14240-8531
IN CANADA: P.O. Box 603, Fort Erie, Ontario L2A 5X3

Want to try 2 free books from another series? Call 1-800-873-8635 or visit www.ReaderService.com.

---

*Terms and prices subject to change without notice. Prices do not include sales taxes, which will be charged (if applicable) based on your state or country of residence. Canadian residents will be charged applicable taxes. Offer not valid in Quebec. This offer is limited to one order per household. Books received may not be as shown. Not valid for current subscribers to Harlequin Desire books. All orders subject to approval. Credit or debit balances in a customer's account(s) may be offset by any other outstanding balance owed by or to the customer. Please allow 4 to 6 weeks for delivery. Offer available while quantities last.

Your Privacy—The Reader Service is committed to protecting your privacy. Our Privacy Policy is available online at www.ReaderService.com or upon request from the Reader Service. We make a portion of our mailing list available to reputable third parties that offer products we believe may interest you. If you prefer that we not exchange your name with third parties, or if you wish to clarify or modify your communication preferences, please visit us at www.ReaderService.com/consumerschoice or write to us at Reader Service Preference Service, P.O. Box 9062, Buffalo, NY 14240-9062. Include your complete name and address.

HD19R3

SPECIAL EXCERPT FROM

HQN™

*Gabe Dalton knows he should ignore his attraction to
Jamie Dodge...but her tough-talking attitude masks an
innocence that tempts him past breaking point...*

Read on for a sneak preview of
Cowboy to the Core
by New York Times *and* USA TODAY
bestselling author Maisey Yates.

"You sure like coming up to me guns blazing, Jamie Dodge.
Just saying whatever it is that's on your mind. No concern for
the fallout of it. Well, all things considered, I'm pretty sick of
keeping myself on a leash."

He cupped her face, and in the dim light he could see that she
was staring up at him, her eyes wide. And then, without letting
another breath go by, he dipped his head and his lips crushed up
against Jamie Dodge's.

They were soft.

Good God, she was soft.

He didn't know what he had expected.

Prickles, maybe.

But no, her lips were the softest, sweetest thing he'd felt in
a long time. It was like a flash of light had gone off and erased
everything in his brain, like all his thoughts had been printed on
an old-school film roll.

There was nothing.

Nothing beyond the sensation of her skin beneath his
fingertips, the feel of her mouth under his. She was frozen
beneath his touch, and he shifted, tilting his head to the side and
darting his tongue out, flicking it against the seam of her lips.

She gasped, and he took advantage of that, getting entry into that pretty mouth so he could taste her, deep and long, and exactly how he'd been fantasizing about.

Oh, those fantasies hadn't been a fully realized scroll of images. No. It had been a feeling.

An invisible band of tension that had stretched between them in small spaces of time. In the leap of panic in his heart when he'd seen her fall from the horse earlier today.

It had been embedded in all of those things and he hadn't realized exactly what it meant he wanted until the right moment. And then suddenly it was like her shock transformed into something else entirely.

She arched toward him, her breasts pressing against his chest, her hands coming up to his face. She thrust her chin upward, making the kiss harder, deeper. He drove his tongue deep, sliding it against hers, and she made a small sound like a whimpering kitten. The smallest sound he'd ever heard Jamie Dodge make.

He pulled away from her, nipped her lower lip and then pressed his mouth to hers one more time before releasing his hold.

She looked dazed. He felt about how she looked.

"I thought about it," he said. "And I realized I couldn't let this one go. I let you criticize my riding, question my authority, but I wasn't about to let you get away with cock-blocking me, telling me you're jealous and then telling me you don't know if you want me. So I figured maybe I'd give you something to think about."

Don't miss
Cowboy to the Core *by Maisey Yates,*
available July 2019 wherever
Harlequin® *books and ebooks are sold.*

www.Harlequin.com

PHMYEXP0719

I hate my boss

My demanding, stone-hearted, arrogant bastard boss.

You know those people in an elevator who click the close button repeatedly when they see someone coming just to avoid human contact? You know what?

That's my boss. But worse.

As I settle in, I notice that my boss, William, isn't around.

He's the kind of person who turns up early to work for no good reason. It's probably because he has no social life—he's a lone wolf, according to my mother, but to me, that translates as he's a jerk with no friends. Despite the lackeys who follow him around everywhere, I know he doesn't have any real friends. After all, I control his calendar for personal appointments, and in truth, there aren't many.

But where is he today? Not being early is like being late for him. Until he arrives, there's little I can do, so I meander to the coffee machine and make a cup for myself. As the

HDEXP0719

machine is churning up coffee beans, the elevator dings and William appears.

I'll admit, something about his presence always knocks the breath from me. He stalks forward, with three people following in his wake. His hair is perfectly slicked, his stubble trimmed close to his sharp jaw. His eyes are a shocking blue. I can picture him now on the front cover of *Business Insider*, his piercing eyes radiating confidence from the page. But today his eyes are clouded by anger.

He spots me waiting. The whole office is watching as he stalks toward me with a bunch of papers in his arms. His colleagues struggle to keep up, and I discard my coffee, suddenly fearful of his glare. Did I do something wrong?

"Good morning, Mr. Walker—"

"Good morning, India," he growls.

He shoves the papers into my arms and I almost topple over in surprise. "I need you to sort out this paperwork mess and I don't want to hear another word from you until it's done." When he stalks away without so much as a smile, I notice I've been holding my breath.

And this is why, despite his beauty, despite his money, despite his drive, I can't stand the man.

Will she feel the same way when
they're in close quarters? Find out in
BIG SHOT
by New York Times *bestselling author Katy Evans.*

Available August 2019 wherever
Harlequin® Desire books and ebooks are sold.

www.Harlequin.com

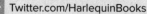